BLUFF

.

PHIL PERKINS

BLUFF

a Mac Burns novel

PALMETTO

PUBLISHING
Charleston, SC
www.PalmettoPublishing.com

The Mac Burns Team
Phil Perkins, Author
Sandra Dube
Front and Back Cover Design and Story Consultant
Marylin Kirby Young
Copy Editor

Paperback ISBN: 979-8-8229-4256-1
eBook ISBN: 979-8-8229-4257-8

Dedication

In prior books I've tended to get a little wordy in my dedications and still manage to leave out some very important people. I promised myself I would keep it brief this time and try to encompass the many people who influence me every day or have had influence on me over the years.

I must first say that without the loving partnership of my wife Sandi this book would not exist. Period. Nor would any of the others. You see we are partners in all things and have been for many, many years. And they said it wouldn't last. Thank you my dear Sandi. What say we keep it going?

Thanks also to my brother Randy, a many talented man. Thanks to my sister Bethany, who writes the good fight.

Now that I'm older, I wake up each day surprised that at this point I live a complex, challenging and exciting life surrounded by complex, challenging and exciting people. What fun!

So, with that in mind, thanks to the men and woman of Libra Sun! Keep on rockin! Thanks to the talented men and women of The Writers of Midlothian. Your writing is inspiring!

Thanks to Lana, Josh, Jeff and all the family members who read my books and cheer me on. Thanks to the readers who contact me with comments and questions about the characters. Feels good.

Thanks to our friends on the island. I won't apologize for Mac's feelings about tourists. Sometimes I am one myself!

Thanks to editor Annie Tobey for publishing my stories in her magazine. Skippy thanks you too (he's one of our dogs.)

Of course, there are many more that I should mention … but you know who you are.

….and here's to Mac and Hero wherever you are.

Contents

Chapter 1

Hortense Mendendo was anything but an alarmist. In fact, she prided herself on taking a calm and calculated approach to life's challenges, whatever came her way. But this was somehow different. In all her years of being an officer of the court, she had never received a threatening phone call. Working primarily on the civil side of the law, she hadn't been responsible for sending anyone to prison. Oh, sure she had managed some lucrative lawsuits that put huge holes in some fat cats' purses, but never had that resulted in threats.

She initially thought about just ignoring the message left on her voicemail.

"We know all about your dad and we know all of the things you did for him. Not a nice picture. Not nice at all. But we can let it slide on certain conditions. Talk to you soon. Have a wonderful day, ya hear?"

The voice was heavily modified such that she couldn't be sure if the caller were male or female, but the threat came through loud and clear. The caller felt as though they had some information on her father or her. Information the person on the phone assumed she wouldn't want made public.

Problem was, she had no idea what they might be referring to. Oh, sure, her dad, Johnny Mendendo, had been a small-time crook working from her native St. Helena Island, but then that was common knowledge. He'd been in and out of the county jail, but had never done anything to warrant prison time. What he had done was earn a nickname that would have suited an actual gangster perfectly—Boneyard Johnny Mendendo. A real gangster might have picked up the nickname by putting people in the boneyard. In her dad's case, it was added to his name because he had run a small scam selling cemetery plots that didn't exist, but the nickname stuck and he grew to like it. It gave his name a certain gravitas.

Despite her father's shaky background, Hortense Mendendo had grown up with deep respect for the rule of law. In college some people urged her to become a human rights activist, and she gave it serious consideration. For some very personal reasons, however, she decided to become a proper attorney. In fact, she ended up joining a Beaufort regional law firm that had a broad background in various aspects of the law, particularly those unique to South Carolina. The firm hadn't hesitated to hire her due to her impeccable credentials—Howard undergrad and then Duke Law. After only a few short years as an associate, the name on the door became Martin, Speckman and Mendendo.

Her dad's comment on her becoming partner was much the same as it had been when she graduated law school.

"That may come in handy."

However, it had never been a factor in the navigation of her family life. She now lived in Beaufort, a lovely bayfront town with many shops and restaurants that drove a bustling tourist trade. It was also the location of the main courthouse, and as a result, the center of the practice of law in that county. Making a move there was just a natural thing. Still, she loved going back to St. Helena and enjoying the company of her family and the many friends she'd made growing up. The traditions of her family ran deep. The food, the music and even the dialect were comforting to her.

To be sure, when in court, Hortense Mendendo was a force to be reckoned with. She learned to set aside affectations, albeit reluctantly, and address the court in a particular way. She showed respect and expected respect in return. She got it.

But back on her island Hortense became "Child". Her mother and father had always called her that. It was still deeply soothing to hear that nickname in their lilting accents. Someone told her long ago that it was the translation of their family name, but she could never find any evidence of that. Nonetheless, Child suited her just fine.

Finding herself just a bit unnerved by the threatening call, she decided to pack up a little early and head to St. Helena for an overnighter. She usually visited only on the weekends, and this was Wednesday, but her parents had insisted on keeping her room always ready. They initially tried to dissuade her from moving to Beaufort. Seemed like a big city to them and brought with it all the bad things that implied. But after visiting her a few times, they came to accept the wisdom of the relocation. And anyway, Hortense was able to treat them to some truly nice eateries.

Arriving at her childhood home, she felt the weight of the workweek and the strange call lifted immediately. Her mother greeted her warmly.

"Child, what are doing here today?" Patrice Mendendo asked, clearly happily surprised.

"Ja, git fired?" Johnny Mendendo said, calling out from his recliner with a cackle.

"No, Pappa, I didn't get fired." She responded hugging her mom, "I just needed a little peace and some good family love."

"Well, Child, we got that a plenty here," her mother assured her.

Hortense sat down at the kitchen table without another word. It felt good.

Chapter 2

Mac Burns couldn't remember a hotter summer. Not here in the low country town of Bluffton, South Carolina, and not back in Atlanta, where he had retired as a detective with the police department. The local newspaper, The Island Packet, had reported that it was the hottest summer in thirty years. He didn't know if that was true and didn't much care. Mac loved to sit out on his front porch and jaw with his friends, but even that became almost unbearable when the temperature reached nearly one hundred degrees.

The extreme temperatures did provide for one of life's pleasures. His girlfriend Shelby Crewe retreated to the air conditioning when temperatures topped ninety. That presented Mac with the opportunity to promote indoor activities. Luckily, the younger woman frequently appreciated the effort.

Shelby was a 38-year-old divorcee whose husband ran off to Florida with her best friend Heidi. Shelby was about 5 foot 6 and nicely built, Mac thought. She had brown hair with blonde highlights.

Mac and Shelby had met when he visited the fish house where the young woman waited tables. Every Friday night he would head over to the restaurant and order the same thing. Lowcountry boil. Soon Mac and Shelby had begun to chat and eventually he drummed up the courage to ask her out. He liked the way the young woman called him "hon" and seemed to light up when she saw him. He knew it was possible that she offered the same greeting to all male customers, but he decided to just enjoy it anyway.

Since that first date, they had been virtually insepara-ble. After a messy divorce himself, he was surprised that he even considered another relationship. But this one worked and he was grateful.

One ritual that had developed early in his residence in Bluffton was the evening drink with his neighbor Richard Percival. Percival, or Percy as he preferred to be called, had spent some time in prison after taking the fall for a crime he believed was actually committed by his employer. That said, he had been corporate counsel and signed many of the cor-porate documents on behalf of the company. That put him in the cross hairs of a fraud charge and cost him his license to practice law. He had yet to decide whether to pursue reinstatement, but it was definitely on the table.

Percy was a little older than Mac—in his early sixties—but the two men had bonded over life experience, and the fact that they had ended up in this idyllic little town near the coast, their careers in the rear-view mirrors … like it or not. Their evening sessions over various concoctions such as Mojitos and gin and tonics had cemented the relation-ship, albeit on a questionable premise. The two men felt they deserved the afternoon diversion and apologized to no one.

Shelby joined the men on occasion once her shift at the restaurant was finished. She was more of a sipper than a drinker, but still enjoyed the experience and the stories the older men shared. She did keep an eye on Mac's intake to ensure he was moderate. That was the caregiver side of her background. Mac never seemed to mind the scrutiny.

Mac was pleased that life had settled down just a bit in recent days. As hard as he tried to retire completely, he seemed to be pulled into situations that looked a great deal like his work with the police force. Rock stars accused of murder, a son pursued by what appeared to be his father for all the wrong reasons and a real estate development company run amok. But, for the past two months or so, all was quiet. It felt really good. Shelby was happy and that made him happy. But in his mind, he heard the words—stand by.

This particular evening Mac was sitting by himself with a Bombay Sapphire and tonic in his right hand and the Island Packet propped up by his left hand. He didn't always read the local paper and when he did, he didn't always accept what was reported. Mac figured every news organization had an "angle", but wasn't certain why he felt that way. Of course, reporting on the improvements on the roadway over to the island didn't seem to lend itself to political opinion.

Lately, Shelby had been talking about buying a house. Mac wasn't sure about that development either. He loved Shelby with all of his heart and knew that marriage was likely inevitable. He certainly wanted to spend the rest of his life with this wonderful woman. That said, he wasn't at all certain about the prospect of moving yet again. He'd suggested Shelby move in with him, but she seemed to want to go all-in on a residence that both of them had a hand in selecting. Time would resolve the issue, he was confident.

Mac had nearly fallen asleep when Shelby pulled up in front of his house. As she approached the porch, he could tell all was not right. Something was on her mind and he knew he was about to hear about it.

"Can I get one of those?" Shelby said, nodding toward his drink.

"Not usually your drink of choice," Mac pointed out.

"Anything is my drink of choice right now," Shelby responded.

Reading the signs Mac freshened his drink and mixed Shelby one of her own.

"So, what's going on?" Mac asked, dreading the response.

"This is difficult to discuss," Shelby said, having a rather large drink of her gin and Tonic.

"It's just me," Mac replied.

"I think maybe we should go inside to talk about this," Shelby suggested.

Settling onto the couch in the living room, Mac was apprehensive about what he was about to hear, particularly given the need to relocate. Shelby was clearly uncomfortable.

"What is it, Shelby?"

"It's about my ex-husband," Shelby responded, her eyes averted.

"What about him?"

"He … uh … he has certain photographs."

"What kind of photographs?"

There was a long pause before Shelby responded.

"Nudes."

"Nude pictures of you?"

"Yes … I'm so sorry, Mac, but it was years ago."

"Are they like glamour shots?" Mac asked.

"No … they're nudes."

"I don't want you to think I'm taking this lightly, but why do you even care? Not unusual with couples."

"Wouldn't matter, except that he's saying he's going to release them," Shelby said, tearing up slightly.

"To whom?" Mac said, not clearly understanding the problem.

"The public, I guess."

"I'm still not sure I understand. How would he release the pictures to the public? Sell them to a magazine?"

"Of course not. Nobody buys those anymore," Shelby was growing impatient. "I guess he would post them on some social media site or other."

"I see," Mac said, "and then, tell people you know where they can find them."

"Exactly. I don't want the people I work with seeing those. I might even lose my job over it."

"How bad are they?"

"Come on, Mac, you know me better than that. Just nudes. Plain old posed nude photos of one naïve girl."

"Did he coerce you to pose … sneak up on you … what?"

"Early in our marriage we were just fooling around. The end. At that time, it just seemed so innocent."

"How many?"

"He may have a bunch—maybe 30 or 40. I can't remember. Seems like a million years ago—another life altogether."

"What does he want, a payday?"

"He says $5,000 and he'll destroy them."

"You know better. This might never end," Mac warned. "How much of a scumbag is he anyway?"

"He can be pretty slimy. Can't believe I didn't figure that out early in our marriage."

"How is he communicating with you?"

"He sent an email with a little sample attached. I've had the same personal email for years. Wish I'd have changed it long ago."

"So, the pictures are digital?"

"Yes. He had one of the early iPhones, and loved that he could take pictures anywhere he wanted. That's what started it all."

"Weren't you worried about hacking?"

"Didn't even cross my mind. I didn't know anything about the internet or much about technology at that point. Shame on me, I was maybe twenty-eight and should have known better. I do now, but haven't given it any thought for years."

"So, he'd have no problem sending pictures anywhere he wanted to," Mac said.

"I guess that's right. Damnit!"

"Does he know about me?" Mac asked.

"No idea. Should I tell him?"

"Not yet. I want to think this over. Meanwhile, let me see that email and the picture he attached."

Shelby reluctantly agreed and passed Mac her phone. Mac read the email carefully, and then clicked on the attachment.

"Whoa!"

Chapter 3

Hortense decided not to tell her parents about the threatening call. Why worry them? And anyway, with the bravado that Johnny Mendendo was known to muster, she was concerned that he would try to track down the culprit. Nothing good could come from that.

Instead, she returned to her office on Thursday morning, and elected to confer with her partners. Most of their questions revolved around how to determine who was making the threats, and how to find the person or people. Her partners were more than willing to pursue legal action, if only they knew to whom their legal leverage should be aimed. Hortense admitted it was too early to call in the troops.

But, how to determine who the enemy was or even if there was an actual enemy? Still could be a prank, she supposed. Maybe even an old friend, who had no idea the boundaries of a practical joke. She supposed not. She couldn't think of a soul that would be that naïve—or that cruel.

The firm, of course, offered the services of the company's investigator. All law firms had people who were glorified private eyes, whose job it was to track down evidence. In this case, Hortense declined the offer, since her perception of Clancy Roman was, to say the least, off-putting. Clancy was a former state trooper, a failed law student and bar owner. That was about the entire story. While the other partners had provided Clancy with what they called a "case load", she had elected never to use the services of the firm's investigator. His methods were suspect and his demeanor condescending, particularly to a Southern black woman. No, she would find other means to an end.

"Hello?"

"Percy, this is Hortense."

"Hey, Child, what in the world causes you to grace me with a call."

"I think I might need your help."

Percy had known Hortense for only a short time but they had become friends and "go to resources".

"Well, now, there's a switch. What's up?" Percy asked.

Hortense took the next several minutes to explain the situation.

"Any idea at all who might be behind this?" Percy asked.

"Not a clue, nor do I have any idea what the reference to my father means. I've never been involved in any of my father's legal matters."

"Legal matters?"

"It's a long story, best told with drink in hand."

"I'm sure that can be arranged. So how can I help?"

"Maybe between you and Mac, you can track down this person. I have no idea where to start."

"Was the call on your office phone or your cell?"

"Cell, and that's even more of a mystery. I don't publish that number, and haven't a clue how someone would get it."

"I hate to say this, but that right away points to some-one who knows you. Someone who would call you on that phone with some frequency. Ring any bells?"

"No chance. My family has the number and maybe four friends. That's it. I'd vouch for any one of them in a court of law."

"Well, at some point, you might have to," Percy pointed out.

"You willing to help?" Hortense asked timidly.

"Of course, I am, and I think Mac will try to do what he can."

"That's really comforting. Where do we go from here?"

"Probably Mac's front porch to talk it over. From your comment, I assume you're a drinking woman?"'

"Does the sun rise in the east?" Hortense responded.

"Then you'll fit right in. I'll have a talk with Mac right now and we can set something up."

Percy was able to reach Mac on the phone about four in the afternoon.

"Hortense needs us to do what?" Mac asked, sensing trouble on the horizon.

"Just see if we can pinpoint this joker, and convince him of the error of his ways."

"I'm retired. You do realize that, don't you? I don't rent myself out."

"Nor would I think of asking her for money," Percy responded.

"Oh, just ducky. Pro bono services which I don't provide. Add that to the fee-based services I don't provide and I'm definitely in."

"I haven't made any guarantees to her or promised a long-term commitment, so maybe we can wrap this up quickly."

"Okay, I guess" Mac said reluctantly.

"I'll give her a call to see if she feels like heading over from Beaufort now."

Hortense readily agreed to drive down, but reminded Percy she'd have to be careful with the drinks. Wouldn't do for a respectable Beaufort attorney to be arrested for DUI. Percy figured it wouldn't do for a respectable black woman to be pulled over at all, but kept the thought to himself. He gave her Mac's address and assured her they would do what they could.

Percy let Mac know Hortense was on her way. In about an hour, he noticed the attorney pull up in front of Mac's house. Hortense drove an unassuming black C Class Mercedes. Percy headed down his steps in time to greet her and direct her to the porch on Mac's house, where so many powwows had been held.

Mac hadn't seen Hortense since she had taken a role in helping them bring a rogue real estate development firm to justice. He admired her demeanor and expertise at not only the law, but human relationships. She was the whole package. If he ever found himself in trouble, he knew he would call her.

"Hortense, so glad to see you again," Mac said coming out onto the porch and offering his hand.

"Good to see you, Mac," Hortense said, taking his hand in hers. The handshake was warm and friendly.

"I understand someone is trying to intimidate you. I suspect that's easier said than done," Mac opined.

"Normally, yes, but this, for some reason, has me worried."

"Well, threatening calls are never welcome, and Percy tells me this call came to your cell phone?"

"Right. That would seem to narrow it down, but I actually took the time to list everyone who I believe has that number. I can't find reason to believe anyone on the list would pull a prank like that."

Mac offered his visitors a glass of wine, trying to stay away from a heavier liquor as Percy had suggested. Wine in hand the three sat down to discuss possibilities.

"If you don't think anyone on the list is capable of being responsible, the next question is, might any of them be inclined to give your cell number to someone else for any reason."

"I thought about that. The only scenario might be recommending me to someone. That said, all my family and that small group of friends would have my office number," Hortense responded, "If you think it's worth it, I'll ask each one if they had passed the cell number along

"Process of elimination," Percy pointed out.

"I'll make the calls early tomorrow morning and let you know."

"Are your partners on the list?" Mac asked.

"Well, yes, but they're actually trying to help. I can't imagine one of them being involved."

"How about employees below the partner level?" Percy followed up.

"I … I don't think so, unless one of the partners gave it to an associate. I guess I'll need to ask that question as well, won't I?"

"I'm afraid so," Mac said.

"I think another avenue we need to explore is the internet. There are sites out there that manage to track down all of one's contact information and make it available for a price," Percy suggested.

"How in the world do they get that information?" Hortense seemed incredulous.

"A young man of our acquaintance at the university tells me anything can be found via educated hacking," Percy responded.

"Then, I guess we have some work to do," Mac said.

"I guess we do," Hortense responded, having just a sip of her wine, "I guess we do, indeed."

Chapter 4

The next morning Mac called Shelby to discuss her situation. She had a later shift that day, so he took advantage of her availability.

"Hi, hon," Shelby answered.

"Hey, girl, how are things going?"

"They're going, but I'm still worried."

"That's why I called. I think I need to meet your ex and have a little talk with him," Max said.

"I don't know, Mac. What good would that do?"

"Might convince him that you have friends willing to stand up for you."

"And it might mean a fist fight. He can be a little chippy sometimes."

"You think I've never been in a fist fight?" Mac asked.

"I'm sure you have. You in the mood for one at this stage?" Shelby countered.

"Can't say I am … still."

"Well, I certainly don't plan to pay him."

"I agree," Mac responded, "that would be the worst scenario. Maybe we just report the incident to the police and let them run with it."

"I think he'd just release the pictures and claim they were his property all along. In any case I can't chance this getting too public."

"The only other thing I can think of is to hack him—hack his phone."

"He certainly wouldn't have the same phone all these years later. Same number, I guess, but the actual storage of pictures and so forth would be in the cloud anyway."

"Cloud?" Mac asked, clearly perplexed.

"You must have heard about this, but these days most people don't have a lot of disk storage on their computers. And, of course, phones never had much storage. Instead, documents, pictures and even email can be stored on external servers—that's what they call the cloud," Shelby explained.

"That doesn't sound secure at all."

"A lot of people say that, but in reality, almost all the data stored in the cloud is encrypted.

"Excuse me?" Mac was still quite confused.

"Think of it as scrambling. The documents don't really exist in their original form, but are digitized. The average person couldn't see them or read them, unless they knew how to unencrypt them."

"Boy, you sure have caught up on your tech talk over the years. That said, I think we'd better leave it at that," Mac said. "My head is spinning already."

"It could still be hacked, of course," Shelby pointed out, "If we had someone with the knowledge of that world, we might be able to find the pictures and destroy them. Erase them permanently."

"I thought the scuttlebutt was that nothing can ever be truly erased permanently. At least I heard that somewhere."

"I think it can be done, but it takes some doing."

"Okay. Let's give it a bit of thought. I may have the resource," Mac said, thinking back to his earlier discussion with Hortense.

"I suppose you know we'll need to involve other people to get to bottom of this," Mac pointed out.

"I figured we would … at least Percy … but please try to keep a lid on it," Shelby said in an almost pleading voice.

"I will. No need for anyone to have very many details."

Mac signed off with loving words and terminated the call.

Once off the phone with Shelby, he immediately called Percy.

"Can you come over for a few minutes?" Mac asked.

"Sure, give me fifteen," Percy responded.

It was too early for adult beverages so the two men sat on Mac's front porch sipping coffee. Mac explained Shelby's problem in enough detail that Percy could grasp the importance of solving it.

"Hmm … tricky situation to be sure," Percy said, staring almost directly up.

"Get that out of your head, old man!" Mac said, only half kidding, "You won't be reviewing the photos even if we find them."

"Pity you say that. I guess you know, if I help, I may come across them."

"Sure, but I don't want that to be the reason you do," Mac said.

"Clear enough."

"You know I have to ask certain kinds of questions," Percy pointed out.

"I know, I know."

"Did Shelby do any commercial modeling?"

"You mean nude?"

"Of any kind, but particularly erotic in nature."

"Hell, no!" Mac said emphatically, then hesitated. "At least, I don't think so!"

"We need to know for certain. She may have signed over certain rights, in which case, we can't pursue this."

"You really think Shelby could have been a nude model?" Mac asked, clearly surprised by the question.

"Mac, I can't even remember what I was doing when I was in my twenties, can you?"

"Not so much," Mac admitted, thinking for a moment. "Well, I'll ask, but I suspect there will be a price to pay for that."

"Pay it," Percy said.

Mac dreaded having to ask Shelby the question he knew he had to ask. Her reaction wouldn't be positive. He thought long and hard about the wording of the question and the subsequent justification.

After Shelby's evening shift, she ended up at Mac's place for a late dinner. He asked the question while they enjoyed an after-dinner drink in his living room. He thought it wise to avoid the front porch under the circumstances. Good thinking.

Shelby's response came quickly and forcefully. She stood up from the couch and glared at Mac.

"Damnit, Mac, why the hell would you ask that? Do you know nothing about me?"

"I didn't know you then, Shelby, and any attorney is going to ask that question. Might as well get it out of the way," Mac countered.

"Then it's done with. Absolutely not. It was strictly a personal thing—not public. Damn!"

"Understood. It's a dead issue then."

"Damn!" Shelby repeated, sitting back down, but obviously still agitated.

"Look, Shelby, I'm an ex-cop. I'm really upset by what has happened to you and I'm looking for solutions. I have to ask those sorts of questions

"Sounded more like a Percy question," Shelby said having a deep drink of her cocktail.

"Can't lie … he suggested I ask it … but he's a lawyer."

"Of course … plus he'd like access to the photos."

"You know him well, but I cut off that discussion immediately. I think he just wants to help now."

"I guess I have to accept that."

"Look, Shelby, we need to buy some time while we decide what to do next," Mac said, "I think you have to reach out to your ex. Tell him you're trying to raise the money. That might keep him at bay for a while."

"I hate doing that, but I will."

"It's going to be okay, Shelby. I promise," Mac assured her.

Shelby looked less than comforted.

Chapter 5

Hortense went about the business of asking friends, family and the partners of her firm if they had provided her cell phone number to anyone else. No one could recall having done so—or so they said—nor could they imagine a reason they would have needed to.

A worrisome thought kept coming to her mind, however. One of the partners had seemingly been hesitant to allow her to become a partner. While he eventually voted yes, his misgivings were obvious. She could never tell if it was about race, gender or just plain elitism. Some firms were certainly old boys' clubs, but she never got that vibe from any of the other partners. Only Daniel Potvin seemed to carry himself with an air of entitlement. Canadian by birth, American by choice, the 45-year-old litigator was good at his job, but not well liked at Martin and Speckman.

There were five partners when Hortense joined the firm, all white males. Only two partners' names were on the door as they were the founders and had the greatest equity. She well remembered how visibly distraught Daniel Potvin seemed later when her name was added to the door. Hortense had delivered stellar results in her first year with the firm. As if to test her, the senior partners had thrown her into some very challenging cases that required many billable hours and appropriate results.

Soon the firm became Martin, Speckman and Mendendo. While she was certainly proud of her work, Hortense secretly wondered if naming a woman—and a black woman at that—a senior partner was to some degree a matter of political expedience. Not that she would turn it down. Oh, no. Too much work went into her career. She settled into her new office and continued to deliver the results expected of her. But the bottom line was that Daniel Potvin never spoke with her again. Perhaps he was exacting some revenge. It would be difficult to prove, but it was worth pursuing.

Even before the threatening call, Hortense had been working on what she thought was a creative idea. The firm had an opening for a paralegal and was having difficulty finding just the right person. They were offering a competitive salary and impressive benefits, but it was a taxing position, often requiring long hours working with the attorneys.

Realizing that Percy was rethinking his work life, she wondered if he might consider taking the position, even for a while, just to get his toe back in the water. Of course, Percy would be the most overqualified paralegal in South Carolina. Even though she figured it was a longshot, she decided to speak with him about it. Percy joining the firm would offer the additional benefit of helping get to the bottom of her recent problem.

Percy was having lunch when Hortense called. She wondered if he could meet with her in Beaufort the next morning.

"Have you come across more information on your threatening call?" Percy asked.

"Not exactly, but I do need to talk to you about a potential course of action," Hortense responded.

"I can be there by about 9:30, if that works," Percy offered.

"That works well. See you then."

A little more chit chat and they ended the call.

Percy was stumped. Typically, Hortense was right to the point, given her packed schedule. This sounded different. More personal. He supposed he would find out the next morning.

There was a knock at the door and Percy could see from the sidelights, it was Mac. Percy opened the door and invited his neighbor in. After offering coffee or a beer, the two men sat in the living room.

"Shelby is pretty torn up about this thing with her ex-husband," Mac said.

"As anyone would be, I suppose. He sounds like a real dick to put her through this," Percy opined.

"I told her I wanted to confront him, but Shelby thinks it's a bad idea."

"Is he prone to violence?" Percy asked.

"She thinks he might be, but that's not the hesitation. She thinks he might react by immediately releasing the pictures. She is reluctant to confront him head-on or have me ... or us ... do so."

"Well, something has to be done or the pictures will get out one way or another."

"Does the threat of a lawsuit carry much weight anymore?" Mac wondered out loud.

"To some people, I suppose. What do you have in mind?"

"Maybe you dust off your attorney persona and tell him you are her attorney."

"Technically illegal, I believe," Percy pointed out.

"Seriously?"

"I think just representing yourself as someone's lawyer might at worst be a misdemeanor, but if you actually tried doing the work, it could be big trouble."

"So, you might be okay just implying you represent Shelby, if I'm hearing you right," Mac said.

"Yes, although under my circumstances, anything could backfire."

"Look, Percy, I'm never going to ask you to do anything that could jeopardize your parole or the possibility of regaining your right to practice law, so let's be careful."

"I know, Mac, but I'm willing to skirt around the truth to make the dude think Shelby has some legal muscle."

"Then, maybe we can put together a plan for you to at least speak to him by phone, if not in person," Mac suggested.

"Well, a call from a private residence or cell phone might seem less credible. Let me think about whether I … or we … go see him."

"Whatever you think," Mac said, nodding his head yes.

Chapter 6

Percy hadn't mentioned his coming meeting with Hortense to Mac. He wasn't quite sure why. The whole thing just seemed odd to the former attorney, and he wanted to reserve judgement and comment. He arrived at the Beaufort offices of Martin, Speckman and Mendendo at 9:20 and took a seat in the waiting area. He felt awkward and out of place.

Hortense came virtually bounding out of her office at precisely 9:30 and welcomed Percy warmly. Having a seat in her well-appointed office, Percy had no way of anticipating the conversation to come. If he had, he might have stayed in Bluffton. Or perhaps not. The situation was that confusing. He hadn't even made a decision to return to the workforce, much less in the legal field. As Hortense laid out how the relationship might work, he saw the logic of her suggestion, but had doubts about how stepping down to paralegal might feel. He finally realized it would actually be a step up from ex-con to paralegal. After hearing Hortense's pitch, in fact, he had to admit it was a tempting offer… and the money wasn't half bad.

"Well, Hortense, this has taken me completely by surprise," Percy admitted, "I really have to sleep on your kind offer, but in general, it seems mighty attractive. Can I have until tomorrow?"

"Of course, Percy, take your time," Hortense responded.

"As long as I'm here, can you give me an update on your threatening call?" Percy asked.

"I've checked with anyone who might have the cell phone number and only have one person who might have been inclined to make the call."

Hortense explained the situation with Daniel Potvin. Percy acknowledged that that turn of events might be a motive to make her life miserable.

"If you do come to work for the firm, maybe you'll be able to put an ear to that as time permits."

"Didn't whoever called you give you any sort of deadline or ultimatum?" Percy asked.

"No. Not yet anyway. There's only been that one call and it was short of details. In my experience these things play out over time, but I'm pretty much in the dark at this point."

"Well, let me head back home, and I'll call you in the morning," Percy said, rising to go.

"Please do. I truly hope you accept, even if it ultimately doesn't turn out to be your cup of tea. We could really use your help," Hortense said.

Later that day Percy decided to discuss the offer with Mac and called to set up some porch time. Mac was happy to oblige since Shelby had both lunch and dinner shifts. He hated those days. He had tried to convince her to only do lunch service, but she had convinced him the money during dinner was too substantial to pass up.

Mac was already sitting on his front porch when Percy arrived.

"I took the liberty of mixing a couple of Moscow Mules," Mac said, "You game?"

"Of course!" Percy responded enthusiastically.

"I don't have the proper little copper-colored mugs," Mac pointed out, "But I think it will taste the same in any case."

"Where did you learn about this little treat?" Percy asked, having a sip and admittedly impressed that Mac was introducing a new drink to their porch sessions. That was normally his job.

"Shelby, of course. She tells me they've become a real trendy drink where she works."

"I'm kind of lost. I see you used Texas vodka," Percy said, spying the Tito's bottle on a side table, "so where does the Moscow come from?"

"I guess just the Russians' love for vodka in general," Mac opined, "But hell, Percy, I'm sure you know I'm no authority on expensive drinks—that is, other than Bombay Sapphire and Tonic, of course."

Percy was well aware of Mac's go-to drink.

After both men settled in and had another drink of their Mules, Percy opened up the conversation.

"Mac, I think I may need your advice on something."

"Advice is free here," Mac chuckled, "Good or bad."

"Fact is, I've had a job offer," Percy opened up.

"That's great, Percy … I mean … I guess."

"Truth be told, Hortense wants me to come to work for her firm as a paralegal."

"Holy shit. What does that involve?" Mac asked, eyes widening.

"Mostly, a lot of research for the attorneys. That said, it could mean going for sandwiches or coffee once in a while."

"Would you be okay with that? Seems a little below your station, if you ask me," Mac pointed out.

"Unless you think of me as an ex-con rather than an attorney," Percy replied, remembering his realization earlier that day.

"Point taken."

"I'm torn. On one hand, I'm dying to get back to real work. Not that the food bank isn't rewarding, but that's not what I set out to do with my life. On the other hand, I would once again be reporting to someone—and the last time that situation didn't turn out so well."

"But you seem to trust and even like Hortense," Mac pointed out, "Am I right?"

Percy paused for a few moments and then had another drink of his Mule.

"You're right. Besides, even she understands it isn't my lifelong dream and might be a short-term situation."

"Then, nothing ventured, nothing gained," Mac said raising his glass, as if to toast.

"Then here's to mother Russia!" Percy said kiddingly, also raising his glass.

"Not so much!" Mac responded, "Not so much."

Chapter 7

"I think we need to end this thing with Shelby's ex immediately," Mac was almost yelling into the phone on a call with Percy. "Let's go meet with him and just intimidate him to the point that he understands Shelby isn't someone to be fucked with."

"I have my misgivings," Percy responded, "But agree we can't let this go on."

"I'm going to get his address and phone number and set a meeting up. You in?"

"Of course, Mac. Anything for you and Shelby."

"Thanks, neighbor. I'll let you know what I can set up."

"By the time we have a powwow with this jackass, I may have my new business cards."

"That would be helpful, particularly if we have to invoke Hortense."

Mac had no trouble reaching Shelby's ex-husband. Mac could tell by the discussion on the phone that the guy was less than a scholar. Mac positioned himself as an investigator working with Shelby and her attorney to "solve the problem".

"There is no problem. I have something to sell and she seems to want to buy. No problem," the voice on the other end of the line said.

Mac was fuming at the response, but kept his cool.

"No matter. We need to meet to work out the details," Mac said, trying to sound as credible as possible.

"So you can bring the police?" the man said, "I don't think so."

Mac was beginning to think this guy sounded like some of the thugs he's been forced to deal with during his career. Remembering that Shelby had referred to her ex as Tommy he decided to try being a little more collegial.

"Look, Tommy, no one wants trouble. Shelby just wants to put all of this behind her and get control of whatever pictures you have."

"First of all, don't call me Tommy. Only Shelby called me Tommy and I hated it then," the man said. "It's Tom or ever better Thomas. Understood?"

"Okay, then, from this point on I'll just call you asshole. Rather descriptive, I think," Mac was growing impatient.

The voice went quiet at that comeback.

"We want to meet to see where we go from here. No cops. Just civil discussion," Mac said. "At this point, you haven't even committed a crime—but you're on the verge—understand … er … asshole?"

"How do I know you won't just rough me up?"

"How do I know you won't pull something on us. It's just a matter of trusting each other long enough to put this situation to rest."

"Will you bring the money?" Tommy asked.

"I will bring goodwill, unless you push me any further. Where do you want to meet?"

"I'll meet you in the lobby of the airport at 1PM tomorrow. That should be public enough."

"Which airport, asshole?" Mac felt as though he had to continue with the tough guy persona.

"Savannah Hilton Head."

Mac knew that on a Saturday the airport would be fairly busy in the afternoon catering to tourists and business people returning from sales trips.

"We'll be there," Mac said, terminating the call.

Later in discussions with Percy, Mac had to admit he wasn't certain what could be accomplished during the airport meeting, other than to continue to intimidate Shelby's ex. Nonetheless a confrontation was called for. Maybe the cop/lawyer one two punch would yield results.

The next day at the appointed time, Mac and Percy were seated in porch rockers, watching intently as people arrived from the parking garage. Savannah Hilton Head International wasn't a large, formidable airport—more like compact and efficient. It featured a good-sized public area, roughly circular with the entrance from the parking garages on one side, the boarding and deplaning ramps on the other.

Mac and Percy had a vague idea of what the man would look like based on information provided by Shelby. Not that Shelby approved of this course of action one bit. In fact, she thought it was dangerous and might make things worse. No matter, Mac convinced her to let him exercise his police background to try to mollify her ex-husband.

Mac was told to expect a man in his early forties with longish hair and maybe a goatee. Of course, Shelby hadn't actually seen her ex-husband for quite some time, so Mac tried to factor that into his observations. Neither Mac nor Percy expected an alternative scene at the airport. A well-dressed man in a pinstripe suit had emerged from the gangway, as if he had just deplaned.

"I guess one of you must be Mac Burns," the man said, as he approached their seats.

Mac virtually jumped to his feet.

"I'm Mac Burns. Are you Thomas's attorney?"

"No, sir. I'm Thomas. Sorry to disappoint."

"Where are you coming from?" Percy asked.

"I don't know that it matters, but Charleston. I had business there," the man responded.

"What business are you in, Mr. uh …?"

"Crewe. My name is Thomas Crewe. You know—like Shelby," the man responded. "And, for what it's worth, I'm a business broker."

"Sorry for the third-degree, Mr. Crewe, but I have to say, you don't sound a thing like you did on the phone," Mac commented.

"Thing is, it wasn't me on the phone."

"Oh?" Mac said, confused.

"No, sir. You were speaking with my good-for-nothing brother, Donald—or Donnie, as he prefers to be called."

"Wait a minute, Shelby thought she was talking with you and had the right number."

"Oh, the number was correct—just not the brother. I upgraded phones maybe two years ago and sadly gave my brother my old one. I'm surprised Shelby couldn't tell it wasn't me, but my brother does have a deep voice like mine. I think you're a much better judge of voices than my ex-wife."

"I was a cop. That ability to listen pays off," Mac said.

"Safe to assume the picture was on the phone?" Percy asked.

"Yes sir, but only the one. The one and only."

"Have you regained control of that phone?" Mac asked.

"I have. I don't think Donnie would have been stupid enough to do anything foolish with that one picture. He swears he didn't. That said, I want you to understand that I am aware of Georgia Senate Bill 78 sponsored by old

Harold Jones over in Augusta—trust me, I looked it up. I believe it was ultimately signed into law, wasn't it?"

"I believe so," Percy responded, having no idea if it had been or not.

"If so, and he lied to me, my brother might be liable for posting someone else's sexual photos without their consent. I think that could be a felony punishable by up to five years in jail, if I understand it correctly. I'm hoping we can keep a lid on that. My brother is an idiot, but I'd hate to see him go to prison."

Thomas Crewe pulled the phone from his breast pocket and handed it to Mac without prompting.

"I hope this closes the matter, Mr. Burns. I long ago deleted all other photos. I regret anyone seeing the one."

"Well, Shelby would have to be the one to decide, but I suspect she would be happy with that resolution," Mac responded.

"Then I will leave it with you and trust your good faith."

Mac stood and held out his hand.

"Mr. Crewe, thank you for doing the right thing."

"Shelby never believed that I was capable of doing the right thing, but then, maybe I've grown up some."

"I'm thinking that's the case," Mac said, as Thomas Crewe walked towards the parking garage.

Mac and Percy stood there reflecting for a moment.

"You're going to ask to see the picture, aren't you, Percy?"

"Mac, you know me very well."

"I'll lay the phone down only for about 30 seconds—after that, it's gone."

Percy picked up the phone quickly.

"Holy shit!"

Chapter 8

"Hortense … I accept" Percy said, even while holding his breath.

"I'm so happy, Percy. I think we'll make a great team."

"I guess we'll know soon enough," Percy replied, "When should I report?"

"How about tomorrow? Can you be here by 8:30?"

"I think I can drag my old bones out of bed to be there then."

"Okay. It will likely be a full day so be prepared."

"Dress code?" Percy almost forgot to ask.

"Well, I suggest a jacket, but don't feel obligated to wear a tie."

"Understood."

As Percy prepared for bed that night, he reflected on the recent turn of events. He now had friends and, in fact, allies, unlike when he had been convicted. During those trying times friends couldn't abandon him quickly enough. He wasn't certain he was making the best decision going to work as a paralegal, but was intrigued by the possibilities the job presented.

As he turned off the light, he also reflected on the picture Mac had chosen to share. He was somewhat surprised at how provocative the picture turned out to be, given how demure Shelby would seem to be most days. That said, the vision would likely stay in his memory forever and come to mind each time he saw Mac's lady friend. It was something about the look in the younger Shelby's eyes. Almost haunting. He wondered if Mac had noticed her eyes. He wondered if that's why Mac had allowed him to see the picture. Was he searching for answers? Was she? Oh, well, nothing to fret about … life is good, he thought. Mac had made it clear that he was never to tell Shelby or anyone that he had shared the picture. Percy would always respect that. But those eyes … hmmm.

The next morning Percy made certain he got up with plenty of time to shower, shave and select an appropriate sport coat. He hadn't had much call for the jackets recently but at least most of them still fit and none seemed out of style. He decided on khakis and a blue blazer—the old standard. Never fails one to dress that way whether at work or at the country club.

The drive to Beaufort was uneventful and actually took less time than he had imagined. He'd factor that into his daily routine.

Once at the law firm, he found his way to Hortense's office easily and unimpeded. He found it odd that he hadn't been stopped at the reception station, but supposed Hortense had cleared the way for him. He no longer felt awkward.

"Good morning, boss," Percy said standing in the doorway of her office.

"Please dispense with the boss routine," Hortense said, looking up from her desk. "We just use first names here. Please sit down. I have an update."

Percy wasn't at all certain what update she might have been referencing, but guessed it might be about her threatening call.

"I got another call today and it was a bit more frightening. The voice on the other end of the line said something like '*we need to move this along quickly.*'"

"I don't get it. What demands have they made?" Percy asked.

"That's the odd thing. None. I don't know what they expect of me at this point."

"Are you taping the calls?"

"Well, we don't use tape anymore, but I am recording them."

"Old school, I guess, but either way I need to hear them."

Percy and Hortense sat together and listened to a highly modified voice on the other end of the call.

"Look, Miss Lawyer … I don't know what the holdup is, but we need to move this along quickly. My partners are not as patient as me. Let me know what you plan to do."

Percy was stumped. It was as if the caller had no idea what was going on, or that Hortense had no way of responding.

"Hortense, I think this whole thing is just a bluff to throw you off your game," Percy opined, "Are you working on any large cases right now that might make someone want to rattle you?"

"Only one, and it's more of an investigation working with the Beaufort Police and South Carolina State Patrol."

"Give me the elevator pitch on that one, please."

"Elevator pitch?"

"Sorry—just means, the short version."

"Well, city administrators in Beaufort, Westminster and Jasper counties and the electrical cooperatives that serve them are getting calls threatening to capture and disable the grid."

"Speak English, please," Percy said.

"In other words, they are threatening to shut down electrical power all across the area."

"Could someone do that?'

"Presumably, if they had expert hackers."

"What are the callers demanding to reverse course on disabling the grid."

"They haven't made their demands yet. I suspect they're still sizing up the situation."

"Okay, but I'm lost on why the authorities would involve a private law firm this early in the game. Isn't it just a police matter?" Percy asked logically.

"Well, Beaufort County came to us, so that we could prepare for any legal action that might be needed. We have several former prosecutors on our team—or did you know that?"

"I didn't and frankly, it gives me the creeps," Percy admitted chuckling nervously.

"Well, don't worry, they won't bite. Anyway, you paid your debt to society."

"And then some, as you know."

"So, let's assume for the moment that your threats are related to the Beaufort County issue," Percy said, "About the only way they gain by shaking you up is potentially distracting you, and as Mac pointed out, I'm thinking that isn't easily accomplished."

"One would hope not. But when they mention a family member, it does give you pause," Hortense admitted.

"I think you can exhale now. I'm convinced that this never had anything to do with your father. Just a crude bluff … very crude. But let me see the materials associated with the electric grid issue, so I can at least advise you," Percy offered.

"I'll have everything on your desk shortly," Hortense responded.

"I have a desk? For some reason, I imagined working out of the cafeteria," Percy responded.

"We have a cafeteria?" Hortense mimicked him chuckling.

Percy was surprised at the amount of detail that was enclosed in the materials Hortense gave him. Apparently, there had been several phone calls between officials of Beaufort and Jasper counties and the perpetrators. The threats had been quite specific. Dates, times and demands. He devoured the material quickly.

Turned out Percy did indeed have a desk and in fact, a small office with a rather nice view of the street below. He didn't mind the feeling of slipping back into the legal world at all. It was his world. The fact that he was now a paralegal didn't really bother him much. He was doing the same kind of work and doing it with a woman he respected.

Percy learned to use the phone system as an intercom and buzzed Hortense.

"Hi, Percy, what's up?"

"I have a theory or two. When can we meet?"

"How about around 3? I have court at 1, but should be back by then."

"You're on. I'll see you then," Percy responded.

Chapter 9

At the appointed time Percy entered Hortense's office. "Please sit, good sir," Hortense said brightly.

"You seem in a good mood today," Percy advised.

"Just won a small case involving a corrupt employer. Just feels good."

"Congratulations!"

"The employees involved got a tidy little settlement, if they can ever collect," Hortense pointed out.

"I guess it goes back to law enforcement, if there are problems."

"Yes, our only recourse. So, you said you had some theories?"

"A while back I had occasion to help Mac with a case that required knowledge of hacking. We found a young man at USC that taught us a great deal about the ins and outs of trying to crack highly secure databases and facilities."

"How is that relevant here?" Hortense asked logically.

"It makes me think we are dealing with one of two scenarios. Given that an outsider would have a mighty tough job of hacking all of the co-ops and or the grid, it could be a total hoax—yet another bluff. Second, our bad actors are dealing with someone on the inside who has the power to pull the switch."

"I had thought about the hoax idea but frankly, not the inside job angle," Hortense admitted.

"My only conundrum is inside of what? There are multiple co-ops, 20 in South Carolina alone. But I think they operate fairly independently. I don't know if they all feed into a central grid of some sort, but I suspect not. If I'm right, the callers can't control the entire grid in one grand gesture."

"Point taken. So maybe our best bet is to cozy up to someone in one of the local co-ops and kick around ideas as to what might be going on," Hortense offered.

"Agree. Should I research who that might be?" Percy asked.

"Yes, and I would start with the Sawgrass Cooperative. It covers all of Westminster County, some of Beaufort County and part of Jasper. Someone there must be able to help."

Percy returned to his new office and began to Google the Sawgrass Cooperative hoping to come up with a name that might be helpful. It didn't take long for him to zero in on the Vice President of Information Systems, a man named Ben Parker. If anyone knew how one might hack the system, Percy assumed Mr. Parker or one of his employees would.

Percy was immediately put through to Ben Parker's office.

"Parker," the man answered sounding considerably more cheerful than Percy anticipated. His picture on LinkedIn seemed to portray a staid, formal man.

"Mr. Parker, my name is Richard Percival. I represent Martin, Speckman and Mendendo over here in Beaufort. How are you today, sir?"

"Doing well until now. Is there trouble?" Parker replied.

"Well, we hope not, but need your input on a rather pressing matter."

"The threats against the grid, I imagine."

"Yes, sir."

"Pisses me off. How can I help?" Parker offered up.

"I guess my first question would be, is it possible to hack your system, your controllers—whatever you call them? Can it be done?"

"Mr. Percival, nothing is impossible, but we have some of the most sophisticated security measures in place in the country. Firewalls, complex passwords, alarm systems. You'd have to bypass all of that to actually crash our grid."

"I was hoping you would say that. And now for the more difficult question. Could there be someone inside working with the bad guys?" Percy asked, knowing it might illicit a defensive response.

"I can't imagine that. Our people are vetted completely and all actions fairly closely monitored. It would have to be someone on my team or over in engineering and I know everyone on both crews. Just doesn't fit," Parker said, not sounding defensive in the least.

"So, in your mind this might be a bunch of hokum?"

"Probably, but that hasn't stopped us from double checking all connections and talking to all of our people. Thus far, we can't find any indication there's been any sort of breach in our system or failing with our staff. Is that helpful?"

"Yes, Mr. Parker, most helpful. And glad you folks are being proactive. In fact, I buy my electric from Sawgrass and am happy all seems secure."

"We hope to serve you for many years to come, Mr. Percival."

"Thank you for your time, Mr. Parker. May I call you again if further questions arise?"

"Feel free."

Percy wasn't certain any new information had come from the call. In fact, he anticipated the answers Mr. Parker provided. It sounded as though Sawgrass Electrical Cooperative ran a tight ship and was on the lookout for any issues associated with the threats. He debated calling another co-op, but suspected he would get the same type of response.

It was almost 5, but he decided to buzz Hortense.

"Hey, Percy. What's up?"

"Well, I have to say that the IT guy over at Sawgrass seems to have a grasp on the problem. They've set up both technical and HR safeguards. He doesn't think what the bad guys are threatening can be done, nor does he think anyone on their payroll could be involved."

"Well, it could be misguided loyalty."

"Maybe, but I didn't get that sense. I'm going to sleep on what our next steps might be, if you're okay with that.

"Of course. Busy first day, eh?"

"Yes indeed, but loved it, Hortense."

"That's great, Percy. I love having you here. By the way Percy, one more thing. I keep getting calls from someone named Bartholomew."

"Oh? What's he want?" Percy asked.

"That's the funny thing. He always calls when I'm in court or out of the office or on the other line. Never leaves a message. Just says he'll call back."

"Might be a sales call or something," Percy opined.

"Maybe, but with all that's been going on, it just seems odd."

"Well, the next time he calls and you're just on the other line, tell the people up front to ask him to hold and see if he does."

"Good thought," Hortense agreed.

By the time Percy got home, Mac Burns was sitting on his front porch enjoying a cocktail.

"Ah, here comes the working man," Mac teased.

"Quite a day today, Mac. Want to hear about it?"

"Of course. Care for a drink? I have a pitcher of Mojitos chilling."

"I would, indeed."

Mac fetched Percy a drink, refreshing his at the same time. When he returned to the porch Percy began laying out the ins and outs of his day. No one had suggested that any aspect of the case he was working on was confidential, so he felt free to share most of the details. Anyway, Mac was an ex-cop and knew when he should keep things close to the vest.

"Are you planning to talk to other co-ops?" Mac asked.

"Not sure. Not sure at all what the next step should be. You have any ideas?"

"Well, the cop in me says you should try to actually find these guys. Have the calls traced, do whatever is necessary to track them down."

"Seems logical, if they are least bit technologically savvy, though it might be difficult," Percy pointed out.

"You eat difficult for breakfast, Mr. Percival. Worth a try."

"Yes, sir. Worth a try."

Chapter 10

By the next morning, it was clear to Percy that he needed Mac's help. Oh, the police were all over the case, but they made him uncomfortable in the first place, and in the second, he trusted Mac's instincts. Of course, he'd have to run it by Hortense, but he suspected she might be okay with it, given her disdain for the in-house investigator.

Unfortunately, Hortense was in court all day, making his day far duller than the day before. He used his time wisely studying up on how all the co-ops functioned and what companies served what geographies. Sawgrass was by far one of the largest in the state and covered a large swath of land near the coast. Even if only that co-op was taken offline, many thousands of people would be left without power.

Around 11AM, the front desk alerted Percy to a call for him. To his surprise, it was Parker.

"Hello, Mr. Parker, how can I be of service?" Percy answered.

"After giving our meeting some thought, it occurred to me that there is one employee—we say associate—that might be worth a look."

"Do tell."

"She came to us from a large multi-faceted corporation out of Connecticut. Oh, her references were stellar and she interviewed well, but for some reason, I've always thought she had some disparate agenda."

"What made you think that?" Percy asked.

"She asked a lot of questions in private about how our product got to market—that sort of thing. She was also mighty quiet at all-call staff meetings. Most associates would be vying for time to talk. Could be totally innocent, but it caught my attention."

"I think you were right to bring it to me. At this point, I won't alert the police, but please email me her name and something about her function there. Is that okay?"

"Of course."

Percy gave Parker his contact information and terminated the call.

Curious, Percy thought. Why would he call me?

The woman in question was one Ruby Wilder. Percy immediately thought that the name Ruby was a bit antiquated for what Parker described as about a 25-year-old woman. But then it was her parents who selected it. She only had to live with it.

Percy set about trying to find information about the young woman on social media. Facebook yielded nothing, but he did find her on LinkedIn. The profile still showed her at her prior workplace in Stamford, Connecticut. He knew nothing about Instagram or Tik Tok, but vowed to get up to date.

LinkedIn featured a young up-and-comer with an MBA from Dartmouth and a burgeoning career in business technology. Her work with the Stamford firm had involved statistical analysis and strategic planning. Quite a resume. Ivy League to mainstream big business. Percy wondered how she ended up in an electrical cooperative in South Carolina. There must be a story there.

Hortense returned to the office at around 4PM and Percy saw to it that he was first to ask for a few minutes of her time.

"We need Mac," Percy blurted out once he found himself in her office.

"I beg your pardon?" Hortense responded chuckling.

"I want Mac's help in trying to track down the bad guys who have been making threats about the grid."

"Well, I certainly like and respect Mac, but don't we have enough law enforcement types at our disposal."

"None of them are Mac Burns. He just has an ability to sniff out the root causes of a case and those who take advantage of any situation," Percy replied without hesitation.

"How much will it cost us?' Hortense asked.

"No idea. I haven't approached him, but I suspect just expenses. I could be wrong."

"Well, see what he says and we'll go from there. I assume you'll coordinate his activities."

"Absolutely," Percy responded.

When Percy got home that evening, he noticed Mac wasn't at his usual station on the front porch.

Percy mounted Mac's steps and tapped lightly on his door. Mac had mentioned that when Percy wanted an audience, he was a little rough on the door. He also pointed out that he and Shelby might be—shall we say—occupied on occasion.

In this case, it was simply that Mac had decided to make a credible spaghetti sauce. He hadn't done much with Italian food since college, but figured he remembered enough to pull it off.

Mac answered the door.

"Hey Percy, how was your day?" Mac said, returning to the kitchen.

"Rather uneventful, except for one thing," Percy responded.

"That sounds rather menacing," Mac observed.

"Depends on your perspective."

"Okay, spit it out," Mac said, glancing away from his sauce to the guilty look on Percy's face.

"I need your help on this case. I've already approached Hortense and I know she'll at least cover expenses."

"Nope."

"Come on, Mac, let's at least talk about it."

"Have you not noticed I've been trying to actually retire for the past two or three years?"

"I don't believe totally retiring is in your DNA," Percy opined.

"Maybe not, but it's in my plans."

"This won't take much time. I'm just trying to track down the extortionists and I think you could really help."

The conversation went on like that for several more minutes, until Percy managed to wear Mac down to the point he agreed to come to Beaufort for a briefing.

"I make no promises," Mac said, "But, I'll listen."

"That's all I can ask."

"No, it isn't."

"You might be right," Percy admitted.

Chapter 11

The next morning Mac followed Percy to the law offices. He didn't dare ride with Percy, as he might be stuck there all day. No fun.

The meeting with Hortense was instructive and Mac had to admit to himself that the situation interested him. He hated extortion cases and those who perpetrated the crime. He found that they were typically low life characters with delusions of grandeur. At least, that was his experience.

"Happy to help," Mac heard himself saying to Hortense and Percy, "Just need to recoup my expenses."

"You're too easy, Mac," Hortense said, "Might be a nice bonus, if we can ferret these guys out."

"That would be alright, too," Mac admitted.

"Where do you think you'll start, Mac?" Percy asked.

"I'd like to see transcripts of phone calls, along with any emails or texts from them to Hortense or the co-op people. Can we gather that together?"

"I would think so," Hortense responded.

"Then, we need to get your people trying to track down the IP addresses."

"Man, Mac, you've come a long way in understanding technology since you retired," Percy observed.

"Trust me … I didn't learn that stuff on purpose. You and Shelby pushed me to the brink."

"Sorry, not sorry."

"Have there been any new messages?" Mac asked.

"Not since last week," Hortense answered, "But they are getting more intense."

"And still no monetary demands?"

"Oddly, no. You have to wonder what they hope to accomplish. I think one of their people is just forgetting that part. Baffles me," Hortense responded, "Oh and Percy, that Bartholomew guy called twice again while I was in court yesterday. It's like he knows when to call."

"Who is Bartholomew?" Mac asked.

"Quite frankly, we don't know," Percy responded, "But the frequency and timing of his calls is starting to cause some concern."

It was "date night" for Mac and Shelby, so he headed back to Bluffton in anticipation. He hadn't been home long before Shelby called.

"You at work?" Mac asked.

"Yes. The regular lunch crowd just starting to head out. Lots of people today," Shelby responded.

"Was it worthwhile?"

"If you mean tips, yes. Had some professionals in who seemed to know how to treat a server."

"Good, then you can buy me dinner," Mac kidded.

"I don't think so. Your retirement is more than my salary and tips—so you buy, cheapskate!" Shelby fired back.

"You got it. By the way, where would you like to go for dinner?"

"I know you don't like to go onto the island, but I think I'd like to go to that Japanese place—OKKO I think it's called."

"Not very romantic, sitting at a table with a bunch of other people."

"But it's fun watching those goofy chefs do tricks," Shelby said.

"Okay, you got it. Are you coming to me or am I coming to you?"

"I'll be over and I'll pack for the night."

"Now you're talking!"

They decided upon a time and terminated the call.

Mac did hate going to the island. Even in the off season, it seemed like tourists were everywhere. He supposed he might be wrong and some of the people were just snowbirds … but still. He puttered around the house for the rest of the afternoon, reluctant to start seriously working on the case Percy had brought to him. He'd tackle that in the morning, he supposed.

At around 7 o'clock, Shelby arrived with a big smile on her face.

"Tonight is my treat after all," she said.

"Oh, what's the occasion?"

"The occasion is the biggest tip I've ever received for a two top."

"Two top?"

"I've told you before, that's what we call a two-person lunch or dinner party." Shelby seemed just a bit perturbed.

"Oh, yes, sorry. Just doesn't come up much in conversation. What did they tip you, if you don't mind me asking?"

"$75 on a $200 tab."

"Whoa—was it two guys?" Mac had to wonder.

"No, dumbass, I should have known you would ask that. It was a nice middle-aged couple. I think they just really enjoyed their late lunch and the surroundings."

"Were they locals?" Mac asked, handing Shelby a glass of chardonnay.

"No, on vacation from Pittsburgh, I think. Really nice folks," Shelby said, sitting on a stool at the kitchen counter.

Mac had only recently purchased the stools. His kitchen had a small but handy island, probably from an update some time ago. That said, Shelby pointed out that no one could sit there while the cook toiled. So, Mac corrected the situation with two bentwood style stools with a comfortable back on them.

Before the inevitable hubbub of the Japanese eating experience, Mac thought he would fill Shelby in on the case Percy had brought him. He went into fair detail about the threats and who was doing what to thwart the extortion attempt.

"Sounds like a lot of big brains are on the case. Why do they need you? No offense."

"None taken. Percy just seems to think I can help. It's only a favor at this point. I don't know what I can do, but I'll nose around" Mac responded.

"You always say that. But I won't try to dissuade you. That never has worked."

"Thanks. And if I ever need a pretty young assistant with big tips, I'll look you up," Mac quipped.

"You know, you really are a pig."

"Guilty as charged."

After some further banter, the couple headed across the bridge to visit the Japanese restaurant that had become a favorite on the island. OKKO was in a small shopping center on the north end called Port Royal Plaza, which housed other eateries, as well. Most were burger and pizza joints, although one offered credible steaks. There had been a rather dingy Sam's Club in the center, but a new one was built in Bluffton which outshone the original by a mile, Shelby thought. Shelby was the shopper of the two. She loved browsing for home goods, cooking supplies—virtually anything that made life easier or more interesting. While she was well dressed, she wasn't particularly given to shopping for clothes. If there was a sale at Belk, she would venture out and usually score at least one treasure, but browsing at the outlet malls wasn't her thing.

Once at OKKO, Mac and Shelby were seated with a group of people who seemed to be a family. A very jovial family. Apparently, many of the comments shared among them were quite funny, as laughter prevailed. Luckily, beyond that they were a courteous enough group, exchanging pleasantries when Mac and Shelby arrived. After ordering a drink and miso soup and enjoying a bit of relaxation, the cooking and show started. Mac was happy their table drew an actual Asian chef. It wasn't always the case. Having an Asian just seemed to enhance the experience.

During the cooking routine the Chef would toss a small, cooked shrimp in the direction of each diner. The hope was that it would be caught in the customer's mouth. It seldom was. But Mac and one other middle-aged man managed to pull it off. Mac was rather proud of himself, and rather embarrassed that he participated.

Once dinner was served and the laughter died down a bit, Shelby asked an obvious question.

"Mac, why haven't the bad guys made any demands yet?"

"That, my dear, is the question of the day."

Chapter 12

As if it was planned all along, the next morning the major demand came. It came via an ad strategically placed in both the Beaufort Gazette and the Island Packet. In each case the ad was cryptic, only saying "Co-ops, listen up, $15 million cash. Will call with instructions."

So, it was a big-time cash grab attempt Mac thought to himself, and an aggressive one at that. Millions of dollars flowed through the co-ops. The demand seemed bold, even ill-conceived. These might not be professional criminals. These might be the kind that threw something against the wall to see if it would stick.

Mac called Percy at his new office.

"I assume you saw the demand in the Packet?" Mac asked.

"No, but the word is certainly on the street, or a least around the office," Percy said.

"Well, they have balls, I have to say that for them."

"I suppose so, but you don't think they really expect to get that, do you?" Percy asked.

"Nope. But sometimes stupid knows no bounds," Mac observed. "Any luck with the IP addresses?"

"Not so far. Apparently, their exact address at any given time is hidden behind a VPN."

"VPN?" Mac quizzed.

"You're forgetting we learned about them from the young man at the university. Virtual Private Network. Most larger companies use them to protect sensitive data.

My theory is that they are calling from the location of a company or organization rather than a private residence."

"Can we at least determine the VPN and narrow it down that way?"

"Pretty difficult. And even if you do, there can be many users on a given VPN. We'll keep on it, but it's going to be daunting."

"Okay, Percy, thanks. I'll try some other tactics and see what turns up."

Mac immediately thought to call the newspapers to see if he could find out who placed the ads. The Island Packet and Beaufort Gazette were housed in the same facility and shared many resources. Mac was put directly through to a manager in the ads department.

"Yes, Mr. Burns, I know those ads. Seemed pretty strange to me when they placed them. But every dollar counts right now in our business," Polly Newman said.

"I'm sure. Can you tell me who placed the ads?"

"Well, of course not. Surprised you asked. As odd as they seemed, there's no crime there, right?" Ms. Newman replied, asking the obvious.

"Right, but they may be working up to one and I've been hired to track them down," Mac responded, exaggerating the bit about hired.

"Nonetheless, we can't be sharing business records. I'm sure you understand."

"Can you at least tell me if the caller was male or female?" Mac asked.

"What makes you think the order was placed by phone call?" Polly Newman asked.

"Was it?"

"Well, yes, but that was a bit of a jump to conclusion. I guess it won't hurt to tell you it was a woman. Young woman, I think."

"Well, thank you, Ms. Newman, you've been most helpful," Mac said, terminating the call.

Now Mac knew that at least one person associated with the attempted extortion was a woman, and maybe a young one at that. As a cop Mac had come to realize that even small bits of information like that tended to add up as time went on.

He supposed that all they could do now was wait for the call to come that would provide instructions on how to deliver the money the bad guys demanded. They hadn't been clear who would be contacted, but Mac supposed it might be Hortense, given the early messages. He needed to coach her on how to respond. A trip to the law offices was in order. He decided to call Percy again to see if she was in and might be able to see him.

She was and could.

Seated with Percy in Hortense's office, Mac couldn't help but notice the African motif. Hortense didn't go out of her way to accentuate her Gullah background, but she didn't try to hide it either. Most Gullah people were proud of their heritage and Hortense was no exception. She had simply mastered the art of functioning nicely in other segments of society and was welcomed in most all of them.

"Hortense, I just have a few suggestions, in case the call about the money comes to you, which I suspect it will," Mac said.

"Well, I certainly welcome the input. I must say I've never been involved in anything quite like this."

"I suspect none of us have," Percy offered up.

"I think the main thing is to show the caller some reluctance to believe the premise of the demands they are making," Mac started out.

"I'm sorry?" Hortense said, "I'm not following."

"In other words, you might ask how you are to believe they can even technically pull off the disruption of the electrical grids they claim they can. Ask them if there is some way they can demonstrate their technical expertise on a smaller scale, so that we can believe it's worth the money to stymie their efforts to crash the grids."

"I see … sort of *put up or shut up.*" Hortense said, nodding her head in understanding.

"I'm not sure what sort of stunt they might pull that would be very convincing, Mac," Percy pointed out. "I mean pulling the main on this building wouldn't impress anyone."

"In reality, I don't think they can pull anything off," Mac responded. "It's more of a stall as we try to track them down."

As Mac and Percy left Hortense's office, Percy could see Mac was deep in thought.

"Speak, Mr. Detective," Percy said.

"I'm just worried that the suits at the co-ops won't take all of this seriously enough. The extortionists are hoping the co-ops will take the threats on face value and just pony up for at least part of the money. I've seen this sort of cheap criminal plot work before. I'd at least like the opportunity to snuff it early in the game."

"If I know Hortense, she'll make the suits understand what's at stake."

"I hope so," Mac said.

"I have to ask, Mac," Percy said, "why do you even care?"

"I had one *this close* to being solved back in Atlanta," Mac said, gesturing with his hands indicating six inches or less, "when a local healthcare system with several hospitals paid an initial demand of $2.5 million to stop the extortionists from burning down certain facilities. No proof, no demonstration of capability—just threats. It ended up costing the system $10 million dollars, and maybe even the lives of some patients, before all was said and done. We'll just never know, will we? All because they rushed to pay rather than play it out as my department had suggested."

"As *you* had suggested?"

"Yes, Percy, as I had suggested."

Chapter 13

Nathan Chadwick was feeling fairly good about himself. He had a dream job as president of Sawgrass Electric Co-op, had married the girl of his dreams, had three great kids and a home in one of the more exclusive gated communities near Bluffton. What more could he ask?

Nathan, or "Chad" as he preferred to be called, had been raised poor in Charleston. Not Charleston, South Carolina, mind you, which might have implied a gentile southern breeding. No, he was raised in a rather seedy part of Charleston, West Virginia.

To be sure, Chad had managed to work hard enough to complete his education at Marshall University and earn a degree in business. He continued to work on his executive MBA and had high hopes of completing it soon, but as he got older, the will to study each evening began to wane. Recently, he had picked up the habit of buying lottery tickets. The thought of a quick score and early retirement loomed large.

And then there was Ruby. He had met her at a conference in Boston the year before. They had virtually nothing in common. Moreover, she was fifteen years his junior. Nonetheless, they found things of mutual interest to talk about and in due course were involved in a long-distance affair. Now, Chad didn't consider himself a philanderer. No, sir. He was a family man. A man of values. A provider. Anyway, Ruby lived in New England—until she didn't.

It had gotten to the point that Chad felt as though he couldn't live without Ruby in his life. And he figured, what good was it being president of a multimillion-dollar enterprise, if you didn't have discretionary control of at least a good portion of the funds? He could hire who he wanted for executive staff, he figured. So, he did. Ruby moved to South Carolina. He set her up in a nice little condo. He had come to find out Ruby had expensive tastes, but he was loath to deny her much of anything.

Young Ruby knew about and tolerated his marital situation and put no pressure on him, at least for the moment. Chad was thankful for that. He wondered how long that might last. As long as his largesse lasted, he supposed.

He began thinking about ways to make it a long-term proposition.

Chapter 14

Mac figured it was high time he and Shelby spent some quality time together. The visit to the Japanese restaurant on the island had been a pleasant, if noisy diversion, but Mac needed a little one on one time with his lady. As he was driving home from Beaufort, he called her cell.

"Hey, hon, where are you?" Shelby answered right away.

"I'm on my way back from Hortense's office. On my way home. Where are you?"

"I'm on your front porch sipping a particularly nice drink. Want to join me?" Shelby responded in a breathy voice.

"Oh, hell yes!" Mac affirmed, pressing the accelerator just a little more insistently without exceeding the speed limit. The cops were abundant on certain stretches of SC 170 after all.

In very little time, Mac and Shelby were sitting in Mac's porch rockers, sipping Bombay Sapphire and Tonics. Mac soon began filling his lady friend in on his day and the very large amount of money the bad guys were demanding.

"You don't think they'll pay it, do you?" Shelby asked.

"They would be fools to pay even a portion of it, but I am concerned they might try to placate the extortionists and settle for something less. They do have money."

"You know, Mac, it is their money and their decision. What's that old saying—a fool and his money are soon parted—or something like that."

"Yes, but I am bound and determined to find out who's behind this scheme, before they have to make that lousy decision."

The couple decided to stay in that evening and have what they called a "cooking party". Generally, that meant that one of them would cook as the other one sat at the island and drank, but on occasion, they both contributed to the meal. This was one of those times, as Mac made a rather special Caesar salad, even if he did say so himself, and Shelby grilled two Ribeye steaks Pittsburgh style.

They took their dinner on the porch. Mac had added a small dining table when he met Shelby. Surprisingly, the insects respected the importance of the moment and sought satisfaction elsewhere.

"Let's go away for the weekend," Mac blurted out.

"Now, you know that's not easy to arrange," Shelby countered. "They rely on me to be there for weekend service."

"The place won't close down if you aren't there, just this one time."

"I suppose not. Where do you want to go?" Shelby asked.

"Well, at first I thought Paris, but then reconsidered."

"What was your second choice?"

"Well, you remember Deacon Martin, right?" Mac said.

"Of course, I remember Deacon," Shelby responded, "I also remember he went through hell being accused of murdering his fiancé. If it hadn't been for you, I really believe he would be in prison now."

Mac, Shelby and Percy had been involved in helping to exonerate the now wheelchair bound former rock star who had all but given up on freedom and life itself after losing the love of that very life.

"Deacon hasn't played live since his time with his band Muscle Memory, but I found out he's doing an acoustic tour with his old bass player, Ronnie Hanson, backing him up."

"Oh, I'm so glad for him. I was so afraid he'd never play again," Shelby said.

"Anyway, they're playing at the Carolina Theater in Durham, North Carolina on Saturday. I got us tickets. You game?" Mac asked.

"Of course!"

"He's got that new CD out now and it's called Porch Rocker. I seem to remember him calling himself that the last time we spoke to him. I'll pick it up and we can play it on the way over there."

"How long will it take to drive to Durham?" Shelby asked.

"About five hours—but it will be good to get away."

"Will Percy leave you alone long enough for you to enjoy the weekend?" Shelby teased.

"I'll just shut off my phone."

"I bet you won't."

Chapter 15

Ruby Wilder was bored to death. Oh, sure, when she was with Chad, they managed to find exciting things to do, at least as exciting as one might find in South Carolina. She was a city girl born and raised. She liked city food. City lights. City smells. She liked walking city streets. She liked city attitudes. She liked the nightlife. She liked the friendships cultivated during her sorority days.

Certainly, she enjoyed the creature comforts Chad heaped on her. Her Porsche Boxster, which Chad called a "nice little trinket", suited her just fine. Her condo, while a little small, was well appointed by Lowcountry standards, she thought.

But right at this moment, on this particular day, she was bored.

When Chad broke away from his real family long enough to pay her some attention, he would try his best to placate her by taking her to Charleston or sometimes even to Atlanta to approximate the society lifestyle she was missing. She had to give him an "A" for effort. And he was a sweetheart for giving it his all. So, she would ride this wave for a while.

Ruby had to admit that she didn't totally understand all the details or even the implications of Chad's plan to make what he called a "big score", or what it meant to them as a couple, if he pulled it off. In reality, she knew most of the scheme was probably just this side of illegal, but Chad kept telling her he alone controlled electric power in the area, and had the right to do with it as he pleased. Her smarter self knew better, of course, but being basically a money motivated person caused her to look the other way when she was asked to do things that perhaps she might have never done back home.

She tried her best to maintain what an old boyfriend once explained to her as "plausible deniability". She figured it was just a fancy name for calculated ignorance, but with her degrees she supposed pleading ignorance might be a bit of a stretch.

In the past few days Chad had seemed a bit more on edge. He had even taken to referring to "them" as assholes who weren't taking him seriously and she knew that lit his fuse. She had noticed that when he walked into a room, he demanded everyone's attention and control of the situation. She figured he craved the spotlight and the respect of everyone he encountered. So, she supposed, if whoever "they" were seemed to be ignoring his—shall we say—entreaties, he would not be reacting rationally at all. Not at all.

She knew that the entreaties would escalate to stringent demands pretty quickly. What followed those, if ignored, was anybody's guess.

Taking all of the variables into consideration, she had considered just leaving—but there's the rub. Not doing so provided the very excitement she was missing. Not knowing what came next was a powerful reason to stay. So, she would.

Chapter 16

It was a beautiful day for a drive. Temperature in the low 80s, blue sky, except for a few puffy clouds. Mac had soft jazz on the radio. He and Shelby had diverse tastes in music from jazz to hard rock to even occasional classical pieces or one or two country hits. Maybe a little Chesney or Toby here and there. Certainly, some Jimmy B. But soft jazz had caught their fancy, particularly on Sunday, sitting on the front porch reading the paper.

Mac and Shelby hadn't driven a hundred miles towards Durham before Mac's phone rang. Shelby knew he wouldn't turn it off and figured it wasn't worth giving him the "what for" about it, as her father would say.

"Mac."

"It's Percy, Mac."

"This can't be good news. I think I told you we were going away for a couple of days," Mac said feigning disgust.

"This will only take a minute, but I wanted you to think about something. I called for Ben Parker over at Sawgrass and they tell me he doesn't work there anymore."

"So?"

"Come on, Mac, the guy was a VP—of Information Systems, no less. Those guys don't come easily or cheap. Companies go to great lengths to find them and retain them once hired. They don't just disappear."

"Well, what do you want me to do about it?"

"Nothing right now, I suppose, but I can't help but think this has something to do with him calling me about that young woman. Just a feeling, of course. When you get back maybe, we should try to speak with her," Percy suggested.

"On what pretext?"

"I'll have to think about that," Percy admitted.

"You do that, and I'll call you when we get back to town," Mac said.

"Say hello to …"

But Mac had already ended the call.

"I heard part of that," Shelby said. "Do you think it has anything to do with the co-op case Percy has you helping with?"

"I doubt it, but it is a coincidence at very least."

Ten minutes later, Mac's phone rang again. It was Percy.

"Mystery solved, Mac. Ben Parker was terminated."

"So, they fired him?"

"No, he was killed. Cut down by what they think was a drunk driver crossing the Bluffton Parkway."

"What do you mean they 'think' it was a drunk driver? Is there no one in custody?"

"No, it was a hit and run. They think the guy was drunk because there are no skid marks," Percy explained.

Mac remained silent. He knew that could also mean the driver meant to hit the man. He also knew that the thought had crossed Percy's mind, since he had used the word "terminated".

"Percy, let's not jump to any conclusions. If we do, we'll just make mistakes."

"Understood, Mac. What should we do next?"

"I'll call the Bluffton PD to see if I can cajole them to get a copy of the accident report. You just sit tight until I call you," Mac instructed.

"You bet. Enjoy the show."

"Mac, you're not going to turn back, are you?" Shelby said, dreading the response. "I had to pull some strings and do some trading to get the time off to go to this show."

"No, Shelby, I may make a couple of calls when we get to the hotel, but we'll see the show and enjoy a break. Things back home will wait."

The rest of the drive to Durham was pleasant and, while Mac and Shelby shared some playful banter, Mac still thought about the implications of the death of a key Sawgrass employee, who may or may not have implicated another employee in what he believed was a major extortion case. He supposed Percy was right that finding an excuse to interview Ruby Wilder was in order.

Mac and Shelby checked into a Marriott right next door to the Carolina Theatre in the center of Durham and found a nice burger joint around the corner for an early dinner before the show. Neither of them had been to this venue before, nor had they heard Deacon Martin play, either as part of his band Muscle Memory or as a solo artist.

Once settled at the ornate theater, both of them were amazed with the amount of music Deacon and Ronnie could put out as a duo, but happy to see them joined by a keyboard player in the second set. It added a nice texture. The third song in that set was called "Chloe". That was Deacon's fiancé's name. She was also Ronnie's sister, so it had to be meaningful to both men.

The song was both beautiful and no doubt transformative for everyone who knew the story. It reminded Mac of certain songs by David Crosby. Haunting, yet engaging. But then, what did he know about music and why were his eyes watering. He'd never met Chloe, but thought he knew her through his talks with Deacon. The man's pain after her death was palpable. But the strength it must have taken to get back on the road was uplifting.

After the show they joined the performers for drinks at the lobby bar at the Marriott and toasted their success on the limited tour of mid-sized venues and the success of the Porch Rocker CD.

The next morning Mac and Shelby headed back home to a tangled web of deceit.

Shelby kissed Mac when they arrived at Mac's home and headed off to her own. Mac immediately called Percy.

"Percy."

"Let's find this Ruby person and have a little chat, shall we?"

"I think that's a great idea and I think I know how we can explain why we need to talk to her," Percy offered up.

Percy's idea wasn't much of a plan. It just involved telling her the truth, that they were investigating an attempted extortion involving the entire electrical grid and basically interviewing everyone. They knew Ruby was certain to question why they would have any interest in a 'small potatoes' player like her, but Percy's attorney instinct told him that playing up to her big city vanity might just make things a bit easier.

Making arrangements to actually talk to the woman proved to be the most daunting aspect of the quest. Apparently, even lower-level employees were shielded from outside interruptions to some degree. After plowing through at least three "gatekeepers"—Mac resulting to referring to his questionable police credentials just once—they finally set a time and place to meet with the elusive Ruby Wilder.

She looked nervous. Very nervous. That surprised both Mac and Percy. After all, she was from the city and even though she was quite young, they both supposed city people had a natural hard shell about such matters.

They had been offered and accepted a small conference room to have their talk with Ms. Wilder. It was actually quite a non-intimidating room with several windows and a view of a fountain a story below.

"Why am I here?" Ruby Wilder asked.

"Oh, don't worry, it's just routine stuff," Percy answered.

"I've seen that answer on TV a million times. Why am I here?"

"Okay, some bad guys are trying to extort some money from the electrical cooperatives and by proxy all the citizens of the surrounding counties. We have an idea you might be involved."

"Oh, shit."

Chapter 17

Ruby Wilder wasn't so much a bad interview as she was a silent interview. She was given to the old I "saw nothing" and I "know nothing" responses. Her demeanor could only be described as calmly recalcitrant.

After doing everything to dodge their questions short of "taking the fifth", the two men gave up and excused the young woman, telling her they reserved the right to visit with her again. Her response was not unexpected.

"Whatever."

As Mac and Percy were walking back to Mac's truck, Percy piped up first.

"Mac, is it possible that she is involved, but basically knows nothing about what's going on?"

"In rare cases, I've seen bit players given small parts to play where the greater picture is hard to piece together. It keeps the real evil doers safe. In this case, I just couldn't tell if she was being straight with us or not," Mac replied.

"Tough kid."

"Either that or a cagey co-conspirator," Mac countered.

"Then, there's that."

When Ruby got back to her workspace, she signed out for a break and exited the business to call Nathan Chadwick on his cell phone.

"Chadwi—, oh, hi, Ruby! I didn't notice it was you!"

"Who were these freaks who wanted to interview me about an extortion, Chad?"

"What the hell are you talking about? Slow down and start at the beginning," Chadwick suggested, himself shaken by the question.

"Two men took me into a room and started asking me questions about the co-op and an extortion attempt. Sound familiar?" Ruby said.

"Pipe down, Ruby," Chad implored her, "The walls have ears."

"I'm not stupid, Chad! I'm outside, for shit's sake!"

"What did you tell them, Ruby?"

"Not a damn thing, Chad, because I don't know a damn thing."

"Who did they say they were?"

"One was with a law firm, I think, and one a cop."

"Did you get business cards?"

"I was so nervous, I forgot to ask."

"Then, how do you know the one guy was a cop? Did he show you a badge?"

"I can't remember … I just can't remember… maybe."

"Look, I want you to tell your supervisor, whoever that is now, that you're not feeling well and go home for the day. I'll call you later."

"That I can do."

"Goodbye."

As had been their routine for a good while, Mac and Percy ended up on Mac's front porch in Bluffton at the end of the day to talk out everything from the state of the nation to the challenges of the day. Today, of course, it involved the riddle of the apparent extortion attempt. Each day they would select a special drink and take turns preparing a small pitcher, at least enough for a couple of drinks each. That is, unless Shelby was to be joining them. Then a larger pitcher would be selected. This evening, she was scheduled to arrive shortly. The drink of the evening would be a mojito. After a warm and humid day, an advancing front had cooled the evening off considerably, and the men were enjoying a pleasant 78 degrees.

"Frankly, Mac, I'm stuck on whether this is an inside job or someone outside pulling the strings on some people inside the co-ops, manipulating them in some way to run the scam."

"I don't think this Ruby person is a good indicator one way or another," Mac replied, "If she knows anything, her knowledge is limited by design. My inclination right now is that we're dealing with someone inside one of the co-ops with either deep knowledge of the technology of the grid or the power to control those who do."

"Parker was a technology guy. Seems like he would have been helpful in that scenario," Percy pointed out.

"If he was willing to play ball. Instead, he pointed out that Ruby was a bit suspect."

"Point taken. But is that enough to get you killed?"

"In New York maybe—or even in Atlanta on a bad day. But here it would be surprising," Mac admitted.

"Maybe it was just a hit and run."

"Maybe," Mac nodded but still had his doubts.

"Lot of maybes, Mac," Percy said with a sigh.

"Yep."

Shelby arrived right on schedule and gladly accepted her mojito.

"So, have you two sleuths put the co-op business to bed?" Shelby asked only semi-sincerely.

"Not by a long shot," Mac admitted.

"We can't even determine what *kind* of bad guy we're dealing with," Percy added.

"Don't you always say to start with the obvious, Mac. For instance, when a married woman is murdered you always start with the husband, don't you? So, who would be the obvious person or persons to start with in this case?" Shelby asked.

Both Mac and Percy were quiet for a moment.

"We were both giving that some thought earlier, I guess," Mac said. "The logical first place to start would be a senior executive of one of the co-ops and to be honest Sawgrass would be the place to start. That's where the young woman and Parker work or worked."

Mac took time to explain to Shelby who the two people he mentioned were and how they might play into the overall picture.

"Tomorrow morning, I'm going by the Bluffton Police Department to see what I can find out about the Parker hit and run or whatever it was."

Mac had made friends with several of the officers in Bluffton and felt as though he could count on them for at least some information.

The next morning Mac met with Bluffton police chief Martin Patterson, a man of around sixty with a full head of gray hair and proper Southern way about him.

"I'm not sure what I can tell you, Mac. In my personal opinion, we're dealing with a drunk driver. That stretch of the parkway is particularly bad with people speeding off of the island and so forth," Patterson said.

"But I thought the vehicle was going towards the island, not away from it," Mac countered.

"Very observant. I guess they did mention that in the Packet, didn't they?" Patterson chuckled. "My guess is the drunk was heading home from some bar out by the interstate or even down by Savannah."

"So, was there no evidence that it could have been murder?" Mac asked.

"Absolutely nothing to lead us in that direction, unless you have something to add."

"No, can't say that I do." Mac decided to keep matters to himself. "So, your drunk just ran the guy down and kept on going? Is that it?"

"Yes, and you have to presume he knew he hit the man or at least hit something. That means his car would be badly damaged and there would be specimens left behind," Patterson clarified.

"I assume you've checked the body shops and so forth?"

"Of course, Mac. Small town or not, this isn't our first rodeo," Patterson said, looking mildly insulted.

"No offense, Chief, bad habit from my cop days," Mac said by way of apology.

"Nothing turned up, but you would suppose the guy … assuming it was a guy … would be smart enough to hide the car away for a while before having it repaired.

Mac looked thoughtful.

"Yes … assuming it was a guy."

Chapter 18

"I think it's time to bring Hortense up to date," Percy said over coffee the next morning.

Mac and Percy had decided that early mornings were necessary, if temporarily back in their routine. So, they took turns brewing a pot of coffee and preparing for the day by reviewing the prior day and planning an agenda. That worked well if they were working on what Percy insisted on calling a "case". Mac hated that because it sounded far too much like police work. He much preferred "doing Percy a favor".

"Let's head on over to the office and book some time with her. I think there's a lot to discuss," Percy suggested.

"Okay, as long as I don't get stuck there. I have a life you know," Mac countered.

"If need be, I'll bring you back at lunch," Percy assured him.

Luckily, when the two men got to the law offices Hortense had an opening in her schedule. The three colleagues hunkered down in her office, coffee in hand, to discuss where they were with the extorsion attempt.

"At this point, I think we can only work on conjecture or educated guesses, perhaps," Mac said.

"But Mac's guesses have years of education behind them," Percy said.

"Don't oversell, my friend. This is an odd one," Mac countered. "From my perspective, it looks a great deal like an inside job, maybe driven by one man."

"One man?" Hortense asked, "Who might that be?"

"I think maybe Nathan Chadwick, president of Sawgrass," Mac responded.

"What specifically points to him?" Hortense kept up her query.

"For one thing, we tracked that young Ruby's first call after meeting with us was to Mr. Chadwick. She went home shortly thereafter."

"How in the world did you find that out?" Hortense was clearly impressed.

"It doesn't take high tech to gather that sort of data," Mac responded.

"Well, that is certainly revealing. It's circumstantial from a legal standpoint, but interesting Nonetheless," Hortense admitted.

"We think maybe there is an affair happening with the two of them," Percy piped up.

"And what leads you to that conclusion?" Hortense asked.

"The tone of her voice during the conversation," Percy admitted.

"So, someone listened?" Hortense drilled down.

"Not us, I assure you!" Percy said defensively.

"It doesn't matter! It can't be used! Good lord, Percy, you know better!"

"But at least we have knowledge of the relationship," Mac pointed out.

"Point taken," Hortense admitted.

"Can we find some reason to confront Mr. Chadwick or is it too early?" Percy asked.

"I think we simply let him know things are closing in on him, as we ask for some indication that they can do what they say they can do," Mac said.

As promised, Percy drove Mac back to Bluffton at lunch. He was eager to hear what Mac thought about next steps.

"Where do we go from here, Mac?"

"We need to get a subtle message to Mr. Chadwick that we don't believe he can pull off any diminishment of the grid at all, much less bring it all down."

"Sounds risky."

"You bet. No risk, no reward," Mac replied.

"Not your reward to risk."

"Huh?"

"Sorry. Just making it up as I go along," Percy laughed.

The men were quiet for a mile or so.

"How do we get a message to him then?" Percy finally asked.

"I suspect the best way is through his girlfriend. She seems like the ideal carrier pigeon in this case."

"Can't wait to understand how you plan to plant the message."

"Nor can I."

Of course, Shelby provided the ideal conduit. She could approach the young woman and raise less concern that she was working against Chadwick's plan. Granted she was somewhat older than Ruby but her youthful appearance made the gap seem less of a problem. But then there was the matter of a cover story.

"Assuming you can convince Shelby to help, what pretense would she use in approaching the woman?" Percy asked.

"I'm thinking she writes for one of the local magazines and is interested in how a girl with Ruby's pedigree and upbringing ended up working at a co-op in the Lowcountry," Mac replied.

"She's not likely to be truthful, of course. Ruby, I mean."

"Granted, but most people are flattered to be asked to talk about themselves for a potential article in a magazine. Anyway, that's not the ultimate goal. We just want to get Shelby in front of her," Mac pointed out.

"Which magazine did you have in mind?"

"Could be Local Life, CH2 or even Lowcountry Life," Mac rattled off some options.

"Isn't Lowcountry Life just sort of a real estate magazine?"

"Hell, if I know. I just saw it lying on Shelby's coffee table," Mac admitted, chuckling.

Mac decided to explain the plan to Shelby later on after giving it more thought and considering any danger that might be involved. He figured Ruby herself was harmless enough but knew nothing about Nathan Chadwick. So, they would have to tread lightly. That said, based upon her behavior after their first encounter, he knew she would tell Chadwick right away about the "magazine lady".

Shelby was more than willing to help draw Ruby out. She showed a preference for making subtle references to working for Local Life since she was a regular reader and knew their style. She assured Mac she could do it without coming right out and claiming a direct relationship with the publication.

The next challenge was to find a way to have the two women meet.

"I'll just call her, Mac. I'll simply tell her I'm doing an article for a local magazine about young up-and-comers and would like to interview her about her impression of life/work balance in the Lowcountry or some such. If she meets with me, I can deliver whatever message you need me to deliver," Shelby said.

"I had no idea how devious you could be young lady," Mac said.

"Only when my man needs help."

Mac loved the sound of that.

With a simple plan roughed out they decided to take the rest of the day off for more personal matters.

Chapter 19

Mac managed to work some magic using his contacts at the Bluffton Police station to get Ruby's cell phone number. He didn't ask how they got it, and frankly, didn't want to know. He did know that having it saved a lot of working through gate keepers to reach her at the co-op, as he had needed to do before.

Shelby pledged to try to reach the woman that evening after her lunch shift at the restaurant.

"How did you get this number?" Ruby asked, after Shelby identified herself as a magazine reporter.

"It wasn't difficult. A friend of yours at the co-op gave it to me right away when they found out I wanted to do an article and feature you prominently," Shelby lied.

"What friend?" Ruby had no friends that she could think of, only coworkers.

"… uh … maybe Tracy?"

"Tracy Renner? I don't think so. Anyway, what do you want with me?"

Mac had taught her that Tracy was a very common name in that age group. Much more so than Ruby.

"No, seriously, I just want to interview you for the magazine about life and work in the Lowcountry for a young, educated woman in these times. I think you would have a unique perspective."

The line went silent for a time.

"Would you be willing to meet me for a short discussion?" Shelby asked, "It really won't take long."

"Where?"

"Wherever you like. Your place or a restaurant or bar—your choice."

"Okay. I'll meet you at the bar at Nectar at 7. I won't have much time, though. I have a date."

"Oh, good for you," Shelby said, "I'll be happy to meet you there."

At the appointed time, Shelby entered the open-air bar area at Nectar and spotted a woman sitting on a stool at the bar that matched the description of Ruby Mac had given her. Her first thought was that she looked not much more than a teenager and so innocent. She almost regretted that she might have a role in linking her to some criminal enterprise. But then, maybe she was only a bit player.

"Are you Ruby?" Shelby said, extending her hand.

"I am," The woman answered displaying a rather cold manner.

"I'm Shelley Williams from the magazine. I'm very pleased to meet you," Shelby sat down on an adjacent stool.

"I still don't understand what you might want with me. I'm really nobody at the co-op," Ruby said.

"Oh, Ruby, you are far from nobody."

"I'm afraid I'm lost."

"To begin with, lots of people wonder what would bring you down here from what might have been fertile ground for starting a lucrative career in New England, to work for a two-bit co-operative in South Carolina," Shelby threw down the gauntlet.

"Well, that's a hell of a way to start the conversation."

"You'll pardon my frankness, but you hardly seem the type to throw away that world for this one. Small town. Smaller dreams. There has to be more."

Ruby Wilder moved as if to slide off of her stool.

"I'd suggest you stay for at least a few more minutes. I think it would be to your legal advantage," Shelby said.

"Legal?"

"Yes. I'm not with the magazine, but am associated with some people who want to protect the grid, if you catch my drift."

"No, ma'am, I don't."

Shelby hated the ma'am bit.

"I assume your date this evening is with Nathan Chadwick?"

Silence.

"We know about your relationship. We assume that's why a girl with your—shall we say—pedigree, would come all the way here for a nothing job," Shelby rubbed it in.

"You know nothing of the sort," Ruby began to sound defiant and again moved as if to leave.

"Ruby, you can leave if you like, but I have a message for you to take to Mr. Chadwick. We don't believe he has any means to provide a demonstration of the capability to cripple the grid, such that we would pay any amount of money to stop his actions. We believe he's bluffing. Full stop. You got that?"

Ruby was obviously rattled, but managed one final statement.

"I have no idea what you are talking about and have no direct contact with our CEO, but if I ever do, I'll deliver your message. Meanwhile, don't ever call me again."

And with that, Ruby Wilder left.

Shelby hurried back to Mac's house to report on the encounter with Ruby. Mac and Percy were on the porch waiting for her and offered her a Bombay Sapphire and Tonic even before she could make a report. She eagerly accepted it.

"It went just as we had hoped," Shelby said, "That girl is spooked. You could see it in her eyes. I almost felt sorry for her."

"Well, you know damned well her first inclination will be to tell Chadwick the whole story, so either we smoked him out or pissed him off enough to cause him to do something rash," Mac opined.

"I'll call Hortense and let her know the status, in case she gets a call," Percy said, picking up his cell phone.

"You didn't use your real name, did you?" Mac asked Shelby.

"Of course not. You've taught me better than that."

Percy returned to the conversation after his call with the attorney.

"Hortense said she thought the approach to Ruby by someone other than a lawyer or police officer was genius. If it is Chadwick, it will make him wonder about who the adversary is—other co-op people, powerful business leaders, you know what I mean."

"Well, I hope it puts him off balance for a while anyway," Mac said.

Mac's cell phone rang at that moment. He could see by the display that it was someone from the Bluffton police. He did more listening than talking.

"Okay, thanks, Chief. I owe you one," Mac said, as he wrapped up the call.

"Well?" Percy grew impatient.

"Just as we thought. Ruby called Chadwick right after leaving Shelby," Mac said.

"I guess that sort of narrows down the list of suspects, eh Mac?" Shelby asked.

"I guess."

Chapter 20

Nathan Chadwick was sorely in need of a break. He was beginning to feel pressure from all directions. His wife and family were nagging him for a vacation, his young mistress for more attention and even for more clarity on recent adventures at the co-op. He could scarcely remember how he had become entangled with the three men who now seemed to hold sway over much of his life.

Like Ruby, he had met them at a conference some weeks ago where they seemed to just be hanging around the peripheries of the social gatherings, dinners, cocktail parties—that sort of event. It appeared that they knew at least a select few of the executives, so he assumed then that they were leaders in the electric co-op community. But much of the time they spent simply standing on the sidelines, nursing drinks and talking among themselves.

He had been sitting in the conference hotel lobby himself having a drink one evening after the sessions, when the three men approached and asked if they could join him. Though he thought it was somewhat forward, his curiosity yielded a yes.

A round of drinks were ordered and the men proceeded to tell Nathan Chadwick all about himself, his life, his co-op, his family, his frustrations in not achieving the station in life he had aspired to, basically a mind dump of facts that almost no one should have had including his wife.

The men shared their names, but Chadwick quickly forgot them in his astonishment at the depth of knowledge of him and his life. Then came the pitch.

The men promised that if he joined their "consortium", he could expect riches beyond his own rather lofty expectations. Freedom to pursue a new and more exciting future. Then as quickly as the men had appeared at his table, they excused themselves saying Bartholomew would reach out tomorrow to discuss the offer. Bartholomew again identified himself and shook Chadwick's hand.

What an odd and formal name, Chad thought.

The next morning Chadwick was awoken by the front desk clerk alerting him that Mr. Bartholomew would like to host him for breakfast at 8:00 in the main dining room. Nathan Chadwick accepted, not fully knowing why.

Entering the dining room, Chadwick quickly identified the man named Bartholomew. While he had been dressed in a rather imposing dark grey suit the evening before, for the breakfast meeting the man had selected a pastel Ralph Lauren Polo shirt and slacks, which Chadwick found far less intimidating.

"Ah, Mr. Chadwick, good morning to you!" Bartholomew said, standing and offering his hand.

"I'm at a disadvantage, sir," Chadwick said. "I don't know if Bartholomew is your first name or last."

Bartholomew laughed heartily.

"Sorry, Mr. Chadwick. My name is Harry Bartholomew. My colleagues love the surname. They think it sounds regal, I suppose. Have a seat."

Nathan Chadwick settled in and accepted a menu from the server.

"Thank you for the invitation for breakfast, Mr. Bartholomew," Chadwick said.

"Not at all, and it's Harry from this point on. Many I call you Nathan?"

"Actually, I prefer Chad. My friends call me Chad."

"And I do hope we'll become friends," Harry Bartholomew said smiling, broadly.

Both men ordered large breakfasts, Chadwick favoring eggs benedict, while Bartholomew decided on a combination of more healthy options, including such things as egg whites and mixed fruits. Chadwick was impressed, but not convinced.

After breakfast was served Bartholomew began explaining what sort of consortium he represented. It seemed they identified executives in select businesses who had the wherewithal to control such things as gas pipelines, airline schedules and yes, electrical grids. They could then, let's say, encourage certain monied organizations to provide funding to keep those services running as they should.

Keeping his voice low as he had noticed Bartholomew doing Chadwick responded.

"Sounds illegal."

"I think that's overstatement. It's more of an insurance proposition," Bartholomew said with nearly a straight face.

"And there's money to be made in this … um … business?" Chadwick asked the obvious.

"A great deal of money, Chad, and you would be the beneficiary of much of that money. Enough to be secure for the rest of your life."

"Let's just say that I'm intrigued by the opportunity," Chadwick said, after thinking quietly for a moment.

"I can't ask for more than that over breakfast," Bartholomew said wiping his face.

Bartholomew assured Chadwick he would be in touch before the end of the conference to set up the next meeting to fill in the blanks. Meanwhile, he encouraged his new business conquest to think about a life of luxury, away from the tedium of everyday business. Chadwick couldn't help but let his mind wander to some degree.

Nathan Chadwick never saw the three men again during the conference, but did receive a message from Bartholomew suggesting a meeting back in Bluffton to discuss a major "project" that required his expertise. In point of fact, Chadwick took the message as somewhat more than a suggestion. It was more of a firm request that he meet them at a designated time at a suite in Montage at Palmetto Bluff. Chadwick knew very well that Montage was an ultra, high-end resort frequented by the monied class. If the men were trying to impress him, it was working.

Like his neighborhood, Palmetto Bluff was a gated community. Chadwick had been instructed to simply say he had business at the Montage.

"Are you part of Mr. Bartholomew's party then?" the gate attendant asked.

"Yes, yes, I am."

"Put this pass on your dash and proceed straight ahead," the man said, snapping a quick salute.

Chadwick thought that was a nice touch.

Soon he pulled up in front of the hotel and a uniformed attendant offered to valet park his car. Having surrendered the keys, he entered and asked after the designated suite.

What appeared to be a service person opened the door and greeted him with a radiant smile. The young woman wore a simple uniform of black skirt and grey jacket with a hotel badge displaying her name—Grace.

After giving it some thought and seeing the three men sitting at a table sipping drinks, Chadwick accepted a dry martini. He figured one wouldn't hurt. The young woman left the room immediately, as if on cue.

Bartholomew greeted him warmly, remembering to call him Chad. He reintroduced the other men as Ben and Carl, offering no last names. Chadwick wondered why.

Over the course of the next hour, Bartholomew laid out a plan by which they would warn the people of certain areas of the Lowcountry of South Carolina that the electric grid would be brought down indefinitely, unless certain demands were met. The men needed Chadwick because they knew that a demonstration of the capability to do the deed would be demanded, and presumed he knew how to craft a demonstration sufficiently impressive to give pause to the leaders of the community.

"I suppose you know that I don't have the personal knowledge of the technology that could do that sort of demonstration," Chadwick said.

"Of course, Chad. But we also know that the people who do, report to you. You control the brain trust," Bartholomew countered.

"As a matter of fact, my top IT guy just died. Hit by a drunk driver on the Bluffton Parkway. That puts a bit of a constraint on the plan."

"Only a blip," Bartholomew said, "We've already found a very able replacement for Mr. Parker, in fact."

"I beg your pardon?" Chadwick said not quite understanding.

"Yes, indeed. It's Carl here," Bartholomew said, pointing to one of the men at the table, who had thus far been silent.

"I don't understand."

"Carl is an MIT graduate and quite a brilliant computer man. In fact, his credentials are impeccable. We've taken the liberty of preparing a resume that should hold up to any scrutiny you might be under, if any."

Chadwick took the document and looked it over quickly. If all the information on the resume proved to be true, Carl would indeed be a dream candidate. He had years of front-line experience in key technologies and served as Chief Information Officer for a Fortune 500 company along the way. It was a company known for technological innovation, in fact.

"The first step is to put Carl in place and get him familiar with the environment and people. He'll do the digging necessary to begin planning for a demonstration. You'll just need to give him, shall we say, access to areas of the business where the magic happens," Bartholomew explained.

"Guys, I really need to think about this. It's a bit overwhelming," Chadwick admitted.

"Certainly, Chad. I think tomorrow morning by nine o'clock should be sufficient. I'll call you then," Bartholomew said, standing.

And so, Chadwick was dismissed and his journey into a much darker world had begun.

Chapter 21

Chadwick hadn't really been given a choice about the consortium. At 9 o'clock the morning after the meeting at Palmetto Bluff, the discussion simply revolved around when Carl would start. Bartholomew insisted on the very next day and Chadwick meekly agreed. He made necessary arrangements as the day went on, telling his staff and the HR manager that he had the good fortune of running into the perfect candidate at the recent conference. It wasn't exactly true to protocol, but not many questions were asked since he was the CEO. Carl took his seat the very next day.

Chadwick had hoped things would settle down for a while, but he knew that Bartholomew wasn't going to like what Ruby had told him about the woman at the bar. He wasn't going to like it at all. And he knew Bartholomew would like it even less when he admitted he hadn't determined how best to craft an impressive demonstration of their ability to disrupt the grid. In fact, for the first time since this whole thing started, he felt fear.

As if on cue, Chadwick's cell phone rang and he knew full well it was Bartholomew.

"Hello, boss," Chadwick said almost meekly.

"Come on, Chad, I told you, you don't need to call me that. It's just Harry," Bartholomew assured him.

"Well, thanks … uh … Harry. What can I do for you?"

"Just wanted to check on your progress on the demonstration. I hadn't heard anything from you or Carl and it has me a bit worried."

"Just a minor glitch. Should be worked out shortly. I'll fill Carl in by tomorrow and we can get things going," Chadwick had no choice but to lie.

"Outstanding. I guess I'll talk to one of you then," Bartholomew said and simply ended the call without saying another word.

Now Chadwick had to think fast. Should he simply pack up his family and head for parts unknown? Should he admit his failings and face what could be some pretty severe consequences? Or should he try to find people inside the organization who may have the knowledge to pull off a demonstration sufficient to at least impress his "business associates", if not the people on the other side of the business transaction at hand. He supposed he needed to try to make number three happen.

Chadwick needed two things. The name of the smartest technician working with the grid controlled by Sawgrass and a cover story about why he would want to bring down their own grid even for a brief time, so that the technician would cooperate.

Repairs. It could only involve repairs. That would be his cover story.

At home if you need to work on your electrical service, you turn off the power. Suppose a major element of the power grid had been struck by lightning or a plane or some such and needed to be tended to on an emergency basis. It could be that the grid would need to be turned off for a brief period. Was that credible, he wondered? Could he sell it?

Chadwick picked up the phone to call Carl. Let him find the smartest technician, he thought. He needn't dirty his hands after all.

"Carl, can you stop by to talk about our project?"

"You bet," Carl responded immediately.

In a brief, but very much to the point, meeting Chadwick explained to Carl the type of person he was looking for and the plan to bring down the grid in Westminster County for a 12-hour period after letting certain people with money know what he was planning to do. He figured that might seal the deal.

Carl headed off on his mission and Chadwick breathed a sigh of relief that the matter was at least temporarily off his desk. Now he simply had to wait to see if Carl could find the right person to do the deed. He had to admit to himself that having Carl around worried him. It was a bit like having a fox in the henhouse. He always hated that analogy but now found a situation where it applied. Carl had a direct connection to Bartholomew and Chadwick had to be very careful not to make a misstep or say something that would concern his business associates.

After about two hours, Carl returned with what he assured Chadwick was good news.

"I have the guy for you," Carl said almost breathlessly.

"Oh?"

"Yep, he's a gung-ho techie who knows the grid like the back of his hand and tells me he can easily isolate Westminster or even a few blocks of it, if you like."

"No, the entire county will do," Chadwick assured him.

"I told him we were scheduling the repairs and we would let him know when to shut down the service."

"Outstanding. I'll call Bartholomew myself."

Chadwick put a call in to Harry Bartholomew and was happy to hear the man seem impressed with the update.

"Good work, Chad! This should move along quickly now."

"I certainly hope so. Of course, there's the little matter of the challenge thrown down at the Nectar bar. How would you for like for me to handle that?"

"Don't."

"Sir?"

"Just ignore it. Don't give it any credibility. We'll just do the demonstration without further comment. I think it will unnerve our friends on the other side."

"I see your point, er, Harry," Chadwick said, "Calling their bluff, so to speak."

"Exactly. We'll just rub it in after the fact. It will be fun. Good fun."

"Okay. I'll get it scheduled."

In his own mind, Chadwick hoped the money people on the other side would realize the demonstration was in fact a demonstration and not just a routine failure of the grid. He did understand Bartholomew's point in being silent at this point. After all, no one actually knew he was involved. Maybe that was as it should be. No response kept it that way.

Chadwick instructed Carl to have the technician plan the outage for the following evening at 6PM. A dinner time outage would get a lot of attention, and even outrage, at the homeowner level. The more noise about the outage the better, he figured.

And so, at precisely 6PM on a balmy Tuesday evening the electric grid in Westminster County, South Carolina simply stopped working. Televisions turned off, electric stoves stopped making dinners, washers and dryers ended their cycles, in general life came to a halt. People noticed and didn't much like it.

Phone lines lit up.

Chapter 22

"Do you think that's supposed to be the big demonstration?" Percy asked Mac on the phone.

"I'm sorry, Percy, what are you talking about?"

"The television news says that the electric is off in Westminster—completely down—the entire county, I guess."

"Well, that can happen if a truck hits a transformer," Mac rationalized.

"I mean, my electric has gone out over the years and I'll see that my neighbor across the street is still on. Isn't it kind of strange when an entire county goes dark?"

"Maybe it's a really big transformer," Mac said, trying to make a joke.

"Maybe."

"I think we just have to wait to see if they try to contact somebody to take credit."

As it turned out there was no attempt to contact anyone that came to Mac's attention. He even asked Percy to call Hortense to determine if someone had reached out to her. Nada. Something just didn't seem right here. If this was the demonstration, why wasn't Chadwick gloating. Unless it wasn't Chadwick at all. Could they have been wrong? It seemed unlikely.

At twelve noon the next day, the electricity was still out to the entire county and the news stations had offered no explanation as to why there was an outage. No one could remember a time when there was such as massive outage without at least an explanation.

Sawgrass Cooperative simply said they were "making repairs" and would hopefully have power restored by 6PM that evening, a full 24 hours after the failure. No further explanation or justification for the interruption of service. Unprecedented.

At 5 o'clock Nathan Chadwick appeared on Savannah television channel that served Bluffton, Hilton Head and the offended county and apologized for the interruption. He assured viewers that they, too, were trying to track down the reason for the interruption and would share any information they discovered when, and if, it became available.

And, as if by magic, at exactly 6PM, the electric in Westminster County returned to service. The residents were all relieved and for a time all was forgiven, except by the leaders of the various counties, who firmly believed they were being given an ultimatum.

Mac was still not so sure.

Back at Palmetto Bluff, Harry Bartholomew was enjoying a particularly dry martini and decided to call one Nathan Chadwick.

"Chadwick."

"Nicely done, Chad," Bartholomew said.

"Well, thank you, uh, Harry. Just took a little planning."

"I think we did the right thing in letting the folks who run the county governments stew in their juices just a bit before we press on, don't you?"

"I … I suppose so," Chadwick stammered, "But who will make the next contact?"

"Maybe just a creepy little robotic voice this time. I think Carl can whip that up for us."

After the call with Bartholomew, Chadwick again began wondering why in the world he had gotten involved with these people. He hadn't had a bad life. Nice family, young if demanding mistress, good job. What was he thinking?

He was thinking about money and prestige. That's what he was thinking about. But now he was under the control of other people he didn't know at all and he had no idea how to break free of them or if it was even possible.

As Mac predicted more than once, Hortense got the call the next morning at 11AM. It was a stiff, halting robotic voice.

"*How do you like us now? Seen enough? Perhaps not. We'll be in touch with further instructions for payment, but rest assured, we can act with pinpoint accuracy if you doubt us any further. Have a nice day.*"

Hortense wisely elected not to call county executives, instead summoning Mac and Percy to an early afternoon meeting to discuss a response.

At 2PM, they met in Hortense's office. Hortense played the recording of the robotic voice.

"About what I would have expected, I suppose," Mac said. "At this point, they want to stay as anonymous as possible."

"Still, we know that this outage sources somewhere inside of Sawgrass, don't we?" Hortense asked.

"We know that the levers that got thrown are there, just not who threw them," Mac pointed out. "The controls are likely all digital and might even be controlled remotely, if you have a savvy enough technician."

"You're not saying Nathan Chadwick is off the hook, are you?" Percy asked, looking sideways at Mac.

"Absolutely not. I just think we need to deploy a bigger net."

Chapter 23

Nathan Chadwick was driving home and taking his time. He didn't have far to go and wanted to make a phone call before arriving. He hadn't spoken to Ruby in hours and needed a fix. Sure, he would admit it. He was addicted. The way she looked at him, the young skin, the look in her eyes … and that voice. Yes, indeed. He needed a Ruby fix in the worst way. But she wasn't answering. Where could she be?

Of course, Chadwick knew that Ruby was a grown woman and could move about as she wished, but generally speaking, she would always answer her cell phone when he called. After all, he provided it for her. He couldn't really leave her a message asking her to call back, so he just assured her he loved her and would call when he could. Lame, he knew, but all he could offer.

Her not picking up worried him.

His worries compounded when he got home.

"Someone named Bartholomew called, Nathan," His wife, Sharon, informed him. His wife had never elected to call him Chad, even though he'd expressly asked her to do so. Fact was, he hated the name Nathan. Thought it made him sound like a hotdog vendor.

"Bartholomew?"

"Yes, he said you'd know who he was," Sharon said.

He gave his wife a perfunctory kiss on the cheek and grunted out an "oh, yes". He headed to his study. He had designated a small room off of the formal living room his "study". He had once read that all men of breeding had a study and he was determined to have one filled with books, even if he had read almost none of them.

Chadwick found Harry Bartholomew's cell number in his contact list and returned the call.

"Hello, Chad."

"Hello, Harry. Why did you call my home, instead of my cell phone?"

"Oh, sorry. I didn't get an answer. You must have been on it."

"…and how did you get my home number? It's unlisted," Chadwick wondered out loud.

"Well, not to me, I'm afraid," Bartholomew said, laughing.

Chadwick didn't like the sound of that one bit, but held his tongue.

"What can I do for you, Harry," Chadwick said, trying not to sound irritated.

"We need to plan next steps. Let's meet tomorrow at Palmetto Bluff for lunch, shall we?"

"I'll have to cancel a Chamber thing, but I can do that if needed," Chadwick winged it.

"Yes, yes, I think you should under the circumstances."

Like an obedient schoolboy, Nathan Chadwick showed up at the appointed time for lunch at the Octagon inside Montage at Palmetto Bluff. While he and his wife had done some traveling and he had been on many business trips, he nonetheless found the limited menu somewhat intimidating.

Even so, he was able to find a salmon selection that seemed ideal for midday.

As usual Bartholomew had been seated before Chadwick arrived and greeted him with a strong, if overly intense handshake. After the two men settled in, Chadwick was surprised to see that Carl was approaching the table.

"Ah, hello, Carl," Bartholomew said, not rising, "Thank you for joining us on short notice."

"No problem, Harry, no problem at all."

"Have you two had a chance to discuss how we,—shall we say—turn the screw, as it were?" Harry Bartholomew asked.

"We really haven't even had the opportunity to talk at all," Chadwick admitted.

"Well, then, let's talk … carefully … now," Bartholomew said, seeming just slightly perturbed.

A young waitress interrupted at just that moment to ask if they wanted a drink or appetizer.

"Nothing now, dear!" Bartholomew shooed her away with a wave of his hand.

Having a stiff drink of whatever he had ordered before the other men arrived, Bartholomew continued speaking.

"It's time we delivered a clear message that we are running out of time and patience with these people and expect them to act on our warnings. I want the message delivered that they have five business days to pony up the amount we've demanded or the grid goes down."

"Sure, Harry, and how do want the message delivered?" Carl asked.

It was now clear to Chadwick that Carl, if that was his name, had a subordinate role to Bartholomew. No matter how hard Harry Bartholomew tried to present the group as partners, it was his game. Chadwick and the other men were just bit players.

"I think it should be delivered in person to Ms. Hortense Mendendo. Yes. That's the ticket."

"But who in the world would carry the message? That's almost a guarantee of a prison sentence," Nathan Chadwick asked.

"Well, Chad, I might just do it myself. Yes, indeed. I might take pleasure in just doing it myself," Bartholomew responded, his attention seeming to drift.

That suited Chad perfectly fine, although he was dumbfounded that Bartholomew would expose himself like that. There had to be much more to the story. He was almost afraid to find out what. He also had to wonder why the lunch was necessary, if Bartholomew had already decided what the next step should be. Maybe he just wanted to circle the troops.

One thing Chadwick knew for certain. He had to do a little research on Harry Bartholomew. He was ashamed he hadn't done so before. He felt certain Mr. Bartholomew wasn't all that he seemed.

Chapter 24

Mac's cell phone rang about 7AM. It was Shelby.
"Hey, girl. What's up at this ugly hour?"

"Mac, this is weird," Shelby said, "I guess I got a call from what appears to be Ruby Wilder at 1AM last night."

"I have two questions. How did she get your number and did she leave a message?"

"I don't know and no," Shelby answered. "That is to say not a verbal message. It sounded like she was about to speak but just holding the phone to her mouth as if waiting for me to talk to her. Then the call ended."

"You are right … just weird, I have to admit."

"Should I try to reach her?" Shelby asked.

"How do you even know it was her number, Shelby? Was her cell number in your phone?"

"Yes, I saved it in my contacts file after I set up the meeting with her. Force of habit, I guess."

"That's fortunate. I guess you should try to call her back then," Mac suggested.

"I'll try right now and keep trying for a while."

"Okay. Give me a call either way. I really am curious to know why she would be reaching out to you at this point."

Mac had agreed to head over to Hortense's office with Percy, so he had a quick shower and dressed for the day in polo shirt and slacks. It was a far cry from his normal cargo shorts, flip flops and t-shirt, but he figured a modicum of respectability was called for.

Retirement had been in Mac's sights for the past five years as a cop, and almost every day of that period he had envisioned sitting on a beach or his own deck or patio in shorts and t-shirt sipping a tropical drink. Oddly enough, in his daydreams, he was always alone. After his marriage had fallen apart, he assumed he would never "couple up" again. Little did he know there would be a Shelby in his life. He was awfully glad there was.

By 8AM Mac was wondering why he hadn't heard back from Shelby and decided to call her.

"She's not answering, Mac," Shelby said without prompting.

"Doesn't necessarily mean anything. Maybe she's already at work or something," Mac reasoned.

"There's something wrong."

Mac had learned that when Shelby had a hunch, it wasn't to be trivialized.

"I'm not sure what we can do about it. She plays for the other team, as you know," Mac pointed out.

"Yes, but I'm not sure she's on the varsity. She may just be a bit player caught up in something. Mac, she's just a girl."

"She's in her twenties with enough moxie to have a boyfriend with money and influence. You'd think she'd know how to take care of herself."

"You didn't see her eyes when I challenged her at the bar. I think we need to at least try to track her down." Shelby was almost pleading.

"Alright, alright. Do we have her address?"

Shelby gave Mac the address she had managed to find and Mac agreed to drive by and try to determine if the young woman was home, alive and well. Meanwhile, he suggested that Shelby try calling her at Sawgrass and let him know if she was successful in reaching her there.

Mac called Percy and explained the situation. Percy asked to ride along and the two men headed out on a mission of questionable value. Within ten minutes of driving out the Bluffton Parkway, Shelby called.

"She's out sick today," Shelby said.

"Figures," Mac smirked.

Turned out that young Ruby's residence was in a gated community. There was a day when all of the gated communities were called plantations in the Lowcountry, but no more. There was now a negative connotation to that word and it had been dropped from most designations. Many communities were now called "preserves". When Mac and Percy approached the gatehouse at Ruby's community, they were stopped by an overly officious guard who wanted to know their business. He wore a crisp brown clearly polyester uniform and baseball cap with the name of the community emblazoned on it. His rather tiny badge simply said "security".

Thinking of the best way to break the stalemate, Mac pulled out his genuine police badge and assured the "security guard" that they were on police business. The man took no time to look at the badge and snapped to a pert salute. Mac was actually quite impressed with that.

"You really need to stop doing that, I think," Percy said.

"What harm did it do?" Mac said.

"Point taken."

Mac and Percy approached the address given them. The condominium community was well appointed. It was a four-story building built in a modern style with balconies and an obvious southern exposure. The developers had invested heavily in the landscaping, including mature palm trees, giving the development the look of a resort.

"Are we going to actually knock on her door?" Percy asked.

"I don't think we have any choice now," Mac pointed out. "She knows who we are. Plus, she called Shelby. I think she's either jumping sides or is in trouble. Either way we need to try to make contact."

The two men exited Mac's truck and entered Ruby's building. All was quiet except for some music playing in one of the units. Percy said it sounded like Sade and Mac said he had no idea who that was. Percy just rolled his eyes.

When they got to Ruby's door they listened intently for a few minutes, but heard nothing. Finally, Mac knocked lightly. No response. He knocked a little harder. No response.

"I'd say she's not home, Percy said.

"Either that or …" Mac responded, only half kidding.

Mac pressed his ear to the door. He heard nothing at all.

"Percy, you're not going to like this, but I think I'm going to go in."

"I don't like this," Percy agreed.

"You can wait in the truck, if you like."

"I know, I know, plausible deniability. Fuck it. I'm with you."

Mac reached into his pocket and pulled out some small tools.

"You come prepared, don't you?" Percy said.

"In situation like this I do. Just something I learned as a cop when the situation presented itself."

Within thirty seconds, Mac had them inside Ruby's condo.

The place was dark even though the sun was shining outside. Mac noticed that the air conditioning was turned up fairly high. He was concerned about what he might find as a result of that. He warned Percy as delicately as he could.

"Mac, I had already considered that possibility. I have a strong stomach."

"Alright, Percy. Just saying."

The two men walked carefully around the condo disturbing nothing. There was a purse on the coffee table in the living room. Mac used tissues to cover his hands and look inside. There was a driver's license, insurance cards and even money in there, along with a cell phone. The only odd thing he turned up was a piece of notepaper with the name Bartholomew written on it.

"There's that name again, Percy," Mac said, showing his friend the note.

"Not good, Mac. Not good at all," Percy responded.

In the kitchen there was a sandwich on the table that looked half eaten along with a half empty glass of white wine. Mac used the back of his hand to determine that the wine was warm. Whoever had been drinking it had likely been gone for some time.

"Percy, it looks a lot like Ms. Wilder either left in a hurry or was taken in a hurry. I think the best thing for us to do is get out of here for now and maybe report this anonymously sometime later, although I have to think it through. I mean, how would we know?"

"Or we can simply let it play out. Someone at her office or her lover will discover she's missing at some point."

"I suppose so. Unless someone over there is involved. Nathan Chadwick comes to mind."

Chapter 25

As far as Nathan Chadwick could tell there was no Harry Bartholomew, at least no Harry Bartholomew fitting the description of the man he knew. He had spent most of the evening searching the internet for any shred of evidence that any such person existed. There were a number of Harry Bartholomew's around the world, of course. In fact, he was surprised to find the name wasn't as unusual as he had thought. A Gospel singer, a man in Nigeria … but no Harry in any way resembling *his* Harry Bartholomew.

While he was searching, he accessed the human resource records for Carl just for good measure and reminded himself that Carl's last name was Munson. At least, that's what it said on the HR records. There were a number of Carl Munsons as well, but none resembling the man he had hired to run his information systems organization. No surprise there.

Now Nathan Chadwick was very concerned. Correction: He was downright scared. These men were phonies. Why should he have figured them for anything else given the scam they had dragged him into? He wasn't a criminal. He was a corporate leader, a community leader … and in his heart, he knew he was full of shit.

Nathan Chadwick didn't sleep that night. He left for his office a full hour early the next morning, trying Ruby's number over and over again with the same result each time. *Where the hell could she be?*

It wasn't as if he could call the police. Oh, no. Bartholomew had made sure Nathan was fully engaged. He would go down with the rest of the crew. Goodbye, career. Goodbye, family. Goodbye, Ruby.

Oh, yes, Ruby. Same result.

Nathan Chadwick quickly changed directions and headed for her condominium. He noticed right away that her car was parked in its normal spot. Maybe her cell phone battery had run down. That would explain why she wasn't answering. He put any other explanation out of his mind. He had to.

Since he had provided the condo for Ruby, he made sure he had the key. After knocking quietly just briefly, he surveyed his surroundings. Seeing no one that early in the morning, he let himself in.

The living room was dark and he heard no sounds. He called Ruby's name in a hoarse whisper. Nothing. He made his way to her bedroom, half dreading what he might find, but there was nothing to be found. Her bed was made and it seemed everything was in order. He checked the ensuite and then returned to the living room. Right away, he noticed her purse.

Where in the world would she go without her purse?

Nathan then noticed the half-eaten sandwich and half gone glass of wine. Now he was growing frantic. It wasn't like he could file a missing person's report. His whole world was upside down now. He had never felt so alone and helpless. He had to get out of there, he knew it.

Nathan got back to his car as quickly as he could and headed out, but not to his office. Instead, he drove towards Interstate 95. He had no idea where he planned to go, but he did know he needed a break to think things through.

He would call his wife later in the day with some story, but right now he needed a respite and the highway provided it.

It didn't take long before Carl noticed that Nathan hadn't shown up at the office. He asked Nathan's administrative assistant if he was expected later, and she admitted that she didn't really know and it wasn't like him to just miss a day without telling her.

Carl decided to call Harry right away.

"Boss, our Mr. Chadwick is a no-show today."

"Why am I not surprised," Bartholomew responded, "I suppose he's onto the fact that the girl is nowhere to be found."

"Yessir, I would suppose so," Carl agreed.

"Tell you what let's do. How about you clear out her place of residence this afternoon. I'd rather no one be jumping to conclusions about where she is, bless her heart."

"You got that southern thing going now, boss," Carl chuckled.

"When in Rome …"

"Yes, sir! What about her car?"

"Change the VIN and you can keep it," Bartholomew responded, "Just keep it out of the view of Chadwick, if he ever returns."

"Oh, I will … and thanks!" Carl responded, while secretly grumbling under his breath.

Bartholomew terminated the call without further comment and began to wonder whether Nathan Chadwick could be of any further use to him.

He suspected not.

Chadwick didn't pull over until somewhere just north of Jacksonville, Florida. He decided he needed to use his cell phone just one more time. He had to let his wife know he was traveling but alright. But he knew his phone could be tracked and he'd have to replace it.

"Nathan, why are you calling now?" his wife asked suspiciously.

"Did you ever consider I might just want to say good morning or I love you or have a good day?"

"Well, not really, but … good morning."

"Good morning. Listen, honey, I've been called out of town on business. I shouldn't be gone long, but I had to leave on a moment's notice."

"What in the world kind of business can the head of a co-op be sent to do?" Nathan's wife responded, sounding downright condescending.

"Many things, but never you mind about that. I'll call you when I get there."

With that, Nathan ended the call. At that moment he truly hated his wife even though he truly loved her as well.

Nathan stepped out of his car for a moment, threw his phone to the pavement of the rest stop and stomped on it until it was in pieces.

Chapter 26

At precisely nine-thirty that morning, Hortense Mendendo's internal phone rang. The reception desk was calling to say that a Mr. Franklin Porter was there for their appointment. Hortense was immediately taken aback. She had hoped that Franklin Porter was simply a bad memory or better still a figment of her imagination from days gone by.

But obviously he/it wasn't. It was during Duke Law. Mock court. Porter was opposing her and claimed she needlessly humiliated him. He made it out to be a racial thing. Angry black woman, decent white man … that sort of thing. Truth be told, Hortense believed he was simply a weak litigator and got exactly what he deserved. But after that mock trial, which she won handily, he never stopped harassing her until they both graduated and beyond. Calls, notes, strolls by in the student cafeteria, where a casual glance sent an almost malevolent message that was difficult to miss.

Finally, nearly two years after graduation, it all just stopped. She hoped Franklin Porter had simply grown up. Now she had to decide whether to see him. Maybe he wanted to apologize. Maybe he wanted to pick up where he left off. After a rather vigorous argument in her own mind, she decided she had to see him, if only to prove to herself that she was as strong a woman as everyone thought she was and could hold her own.

"See him in."

Hortense recognized the man immediately. Oh, he was, as they say, somewhat thicker and certainly had more gray hair, but it was definitely Franklin Porter. He offered his hand.

"Under the circumstances, Franklin, you'll forgive me if I defer the handshake for the moment. Chalk it up to the pandemic, if you'd rather," Hortense offered.

"No need. I get it," Porter said, being seated.

"What is your business here?"

"Just like in days past, you get right to the point, don't you, Hortense?"

"No point in wasting time. You had no appointment."

"I just came here to tell you, it's me."

"It's you what?" Hortense asked.

"Me behind the electric co-op business," Porter admitted. "Oh, don't bother calling the police. No crime has yet been committed and I'll be gone in a moment. I just wanted you to know that it's me and I am very serious about our demands. You see I've switched sides and I'm very good at what I do."

"Wait, just a minute," Hortense said reaching for her phone.

"Have a lovely day," Porter said, exiting her office.

Hortense didn't call the police, she called Percy in his office.

"Can you come over here, please. I have news."

Percy headed directly to Hortense's office.

"It's not Nathan Chadwick driving this mess after all," Hortense said.

"What?"

Hortense laid out the entire story, including the Duke Law mock trial beginnings.

"That's an awfully long time to hold a grudge," Percy said.

"Thanks for reminding me that I'm getting old," Hortense said ironically.

"That aside, what does your story have to do with the extortion?"

"I suspect it's no coincidence. I'm thinking he looked for a setup where he could make some money and have fun harassing an old nemesis at the same time."

"So, I guess we should try tracking down this Porter guy then?" Percy asked.

"Trust me, Percy, he's not going to be Franklin Porter anymore. He's too clever for that."

"Well, I'm going to bring Mac up to date anyway. He'll have some ideas. Meanwhile. let me tell you about this Ruby Wilder person … but I have to leave out some of the details."

"I'm sure you do," Hortense said, looking at Percy knowingly.

Percy told her enough to make her understand that he and Mac believed she was missing and perhaps the victim of foul play, although it was just a theory.

"Damn, Percy, you have to be careful. You represent the firm now."

"I know, Hortense. Care was taken."

Percy called Mac when he got back to his office and filled him in on the Porter matter. Mac informed him that Nathan Chadwick may have himself gone missing.

"What? How did you come across that information?"

"Funny what you can learn when you simply call his secretary or whatever you call them these days. She said she had no idea where he was and sounded none too happy. Might just be coincidence, of course."

"I don't know, Mac, it all seems like a weird pattern is forming, doesn't it?"

"I have to admit it does."

"Drinks at 5:30?" Percy asked.

"To be sure."

When Percy arrived later for the traditional imbibement, Mac and Shelby were already on Mac's porch.

"Are Moscow Mules to your liking this evening, Mr. Percival?" Mac asked.

"That's a great choice for this evening," Percy responded, then gallantly bent forward to kiss Shelby's hand.

"Hey, watch it, buddy," Mac said kiddingly.

"Come on, Mac, Shelby knows my heart is pure." Percy replied.

"I know no such thing," Shelby laughed.

"Oh, well, I try," Percy shrugged.

"I wonder if we should just start at the beginning of this whole co-op thing and try to make the pieces fit," Mac suggested.

"I don't think we have any choice," Percy agreed, "But we have a new wrinkle. This Porter guy likely made the initial threats to Hortense."

It took some time to bring Shelby up to date on all the nuances of Hortense's ordeal, how it might relate to the co-op extortion and how Porter may have factored into each. Once done the three sat back to try to make sense of it all.

The mules did little to help.

Chapter 27

"We need to find Chadwick!" Bartholomew was virtually yelling into his phone.

Harry Bartholomew had just been made aware that Nathan Chadwick had apparently left town, even though his people had been told to keep an eye on him.

"What do you mean he got past you?" Bartholomew was incredulous at what he was hearing. He had handpicked the people that worked for him and expected perfect results in whatever they were asked to do. Losing Chadwick was less than perfect.

"No matter. Find him. Trace his phone. Do whatever it takes to find him and bring him to me." End of call.

Still seething Bartholomew went back to his meal. He had two projects working. Bringing in some pocket change, as he called it, from the good people in the Lowcountry and bringing his old classmate down once and for all. If things worked out his way, both projects might be accomplished in concert, with Hortense taking the fall for the debacle that he planned for the co-ops. Wouldn't that be sweet.

Bartholomew hadn't been Franklin Porter for many years. He'd been other people to be certain. Before Harry, he supposed his favorite was Derek Benjamin, an investment banker from Boston. He was able to pull together some very credible credentials for Mr. Benjamin, that allowed him to run in monied circles and enjoy a social life that included some attractive and cultured young ladies.

Yes, he rather missed Mr. Benjamin. But ultimately, you just have to move on.

Of course, Harry Bartholomew had done well for himself as well … on paper. He had created a background as a real estate investor from Florida who built, managed and then sold resorts. In the process, he had signed branding deals with music and sports stars that yielded well for both him and his partners … on paper.

He was almost at the point of moving on yet again, but needed some capital to make things happen. He'd actually come up with the idea of threatening the electric grid one night as he was watching a football game and lost power during an ice storm. Between curse words, he realized how crippling power outages tended to be. So, he pulled aside his little black book that kept track of little black ideas of how one might extort money from people, and decided to set up a project sometime in the future. Of course, his little black book was actually on his little black smart phone, but then, times had changed.

He realized that Chadwick was a key player in making this project work. If he was spooked enough to run, the entire thing might blow up. Sweet talking might be in order, if his inept people could even find the man. Putting the poor schmuck out of his misery would serve no purpose at all at this point, unless he planned to go to the police. But what could he offer up in terms of proving a crime? After all, Harry Bartholomew barely existed in this part of the country. No address. No trail. No crime. Nada. So, reasoning with the man was worth a try. Yessir, worth a try.

Meanwhile, Nathan Chadwick had made it to Miami. He wasn't sure where to go from there but suspected that the population of Dade County provided adequate cover for now. He checked into a second-rate motel under the name Herbert Jenkins and settled down to think and sleep, although the thought of bedbugs kept him awake for a good bit of the night. None seemed to trouble him.

The next morning, he showered, dressed and drove to a nearby CVS to buy a cell phone that couldn't be traced, so that he could call his wife from time to time. It wouldn't serve his purposes for her to report him missing. He'd just tell her that his phone was lost at a rest stop. She would have no reason not to believe him.

Nathan was surprised at the price of the phone, but paid cash and returned to his car. He called his wife and explained why he was calling from a different number. She sounded skeptical but accepted the story after a minute or two. However, she had her own story to share. Seems as though someone named Carl had been by looking for him. Apparently, the people at the office were concerned about him. His wife couldn't quite understand why that would be if he was away on business.

"Look, honey, I don't report to them, they report to me. I don't tell them about everything I do. I'll call Carl later," Nathan attempted to assuage her concerns. He hoped it worked.

Carl showing up at his home meant that Bartholomew was actively looking for him. He had hoped that he had slipped away quietly and that his departure wasn't noticed. Fat chance. For a fleeting moment, he wondered what it would take to get into Cuba … but knew that was pure folly.

It was at that moment that Nathan made a critical decision. He had to make a clean break. He wasn't a criminal.

He wasn't a gangster. He's always lived a clean life. How in the world did he end up on the run?

No, sir. This was no life for a man like him. He had to turn this all around. He had called his wife. He had other calls to make. Calls that could change his life for the better … and maybe just save his life.

Nathan picked up his phone and dialed the number he never anticipated dialing.

Chapter 28

"Percy, I think you should come over to my office. I just got the strangest voice mail. I think you should hear it," Hortense said.

"Be right there."

When Percy entered the room, it was just in time to hear a man's voice saying "*please call me back at this number right away. It's rather urgent.*"

"Who was that, Hortense?" Percy asked.

"I don't know who it really was, but the person claimed to be Nathan Chadwick."

"More threats, but this time right from the horse's mouth?" Percy surmised.

"Anything but, if it was really him. He claims to want to scuttle the entire scheme or at least get away from it."

"Let me hear the message, please," Percy asked of her.

Hortense pushed the playback button. A timid sounding voice was heard.

"*Ms. Mendendo, you don't know me directly, but I suspect you know me by reputation and not my reputation as a businessman. This is Nathan Chadwick. I got mixed up with some people that I shouldn't have and now I'd like to put that mistake behind me. I think I need your help to do that. Please call me back at this number right away. It's rather urgent.*"

"Well, whoever it is certainly sounds under duress, even scared," Percy commented.

"Do you suppose I should call him back?" Hortense asked.

"No, quite frankly, I think Mac should."

"I couldn't agree more. If I do, it might even be treading on ethics issues."

"I'll call Mac right now."

Percy pulled the cell phone from his pocket and rang Mac. He figured the ex-cop would be home preparing for a nice evening with Shelby, but also knew he would want to know about this odd development.

"Hey, Percy, what's up?" Mac said, recognizing Percy's number immediately.

"Well, Mac, I have something here I need you to listen to."

"That sounds mysterious enough."

"Hold on a minute while I restart this message."

Percy held his phone to the speaker and played the message for Mac.

"What do you think?" Percy asked Mac.

"Play that for me again, Percy."

"Sure."

Percy repositioned the phone and played the message again.

"So?"

Mac thought for a minute and replied.

"That is one distressed man … that's pretty clear. But there's no way to tell who it is," Mac pointed out. "Why did you want me to hear it?"

"Because Hortense and I think it would be better if you returned the call."

"I understand why. I assume Hortense's system captured the number. Text it to me and I'll see if he'll speak to me. Maybe I can draw the guy out, whoever he is."

"Thanks, Mac. I know Hortense appreciates the help."

Nathan Chadwick wasn't startled to receive a call on his new phone, since he had asked Hortense Mendendo to call, but he was puzzled at the incoming number. He surmised it must be her cell phone.

"Uh, hello."

"Is this Mr. Chadwick?"

Nathan wasn't expecting a man's voice and wasn't taking any chances. He immediately terminated the call. In less than a minute he received a text.

"*I'm calling for Hortense Mendendo. When I call again, please stay on the line.*"

When his phone rang again, he answered.

"Yes."

"Mr. Chadwick, or whoever you are, my name is Mac Burns and I work with Ms. Mendendo. I'm hoping there is some way you can establish your identity. If you can, we may be able to help you."

"Why would I lie about being Nathan Chadwick?"

"There have been quite a lot of lies going around … why not one more?"

"Look, Mr. … uh … Burns, I'm in trouble here. How can I make you believe I am the man I say I am?'

"I have an idea, but it will make you uncomfortable."

"Try me."

"Tell me the name of your mistress."

Silence and then …

"I beg your pardon. I have no mistress!"

"Alright then, sir … have a nice day," Mac said, hesitating just for moment.

"Damn it. Ruby. Ruby Wilder."

"Then, hello, Mr. Chadwick. How can we help you … and what are you offering in return?"

Even as Mac was talking to Nathan Chadwick, Bartholomew was stewing in his juices. Every hour on the hour, he would call Carl for an update on locating the CEO of Sawgrass. Bartholomew just hated loose ends. Hated them. And in this case, he couldn't proceed with his overall plan for the grid unless he reined in this wayward son.

Carl tried assuring his boss that it was only a matter of time until Chadwick would make a mistake and they would have him under control. After all, he was just a puny businessman, not a seasoned criminal. Not someone accustomed to playing cat and mouse. He would slip up, Carl figured. But Bartholomew kept raising his voice, to the point where Carl worried he would have a stroke. While it would shut him up, it didn't serve anyone's purposes to cut off the source of funding for a lifestyle Carl was beginning to relish.

Carl didn't mind many of the duties Bartholomew laid out for him. Most were just administrative in nature. Lately, it had mostly been keeping track of Chadwick, managing the grid demonstration project, and playing the part of the top IT executive at Sawgrass. But terminating the girl. That sort of thing bothered him. He didn't think she knew much about anything and therefore, didn't deserve to be eliminated in the way she was.

At least she was dead for all intents and purposes, when she went into the river. At least, he assumed so. At least.

Chapter 29

Even though Mac established that Nathan Chadwick was talking to him using a burner phone, he didn't much like conversing over the open airwaves. High technology being what it was, he always assumed anything could be intercepted. That said, they stayed connected long enough for Mac to gather that the man was on the run and in fear for his life. Chadwick figured, and Mac had no reason to disbelieve, that the extortionist that Chadwick called Bartholomew might also be a killer. After all, no one had heard from Ruby Wilder in quite some time and Mac and Chadwick agreed there might be motive for her to disappear permanently.

Mac had to think about next steps and asked Chadwick if he felt safe enough to rest for a few hours while Mac thought things through. Chadwick assured him he would keep his head down for a short while, but only for a short while before moving on.

Once off the phone with Chadwick, he called Percy to see if he was coming directly home after office hours.

"Sure. I'll be there by 5:30," Percy told him.

"I want to spend some time bringing you up to date, and talking about how we might go about bringing this whole thing to a close," Mac said.

"You buying?" Percy teased.

"Don't I usually?"

"Ha! See you shortly!"

Right on schedule Percy pulled up and right behind him Shelby. Mac wasn't necessarily expecting her, but was glad to see her anyway.

"I read somewhere yesterday that it was improper to serve Bloody Mary's after midday," Mac said. "So naturally, I whipped up a pitcher."

"You rebel, you!" Shelby laughed.

"Guilty as charged," Mac agreed handing out the drinks.

Shelby hadn't heard much about the co-op extortion situation for a while and obviously knew nothing about the recent call from Nathan Chadwick. Mac and Percy took turns bringing the story forward. Both men knew that Shelby had an innate ability to pick up on nuances of stories that they tended to miss.

"So, why do you suppose this man has so completely turned around at this point?" Shelby asked.

"Based on my conversation with him, I think he thinks the people he's been associated with are a great deal more dangerous than he thought, and that he and his family are in real danger," Mac said.

'What makes him think that?" Shelby followed up.

"He's been trying to reach Ruby Wilder for a while with no luck and says she always returns his calls. I hate to admit this, but we went to her condo and it looked like she was spirited away quickly," Mac explained.

"But interestingly enough, her car was still parked in the parking lot," Percy added.

"Chadwick thinks Bartholomew had her killed and that maybe he's next," Mac said.

"Damn, that name keeps popping up. Why would he be calling Hortense … if it's even him," Percy commented.

"Who knows? But Ruby was definitely in his way, I think. Seems ruthless at best," Mac said.

"Well, that call from her number freaked me out, even though she didn't speak," Shelby reminded them.

"Right now, I think we have two goals. Keep Chadwick out of harm's way and use him as a conduit to bring down the people trying to extort money from the co-ops and the people who subscribe to them," Mac offered up.

"Mac, is the threat to bring down the grid itself a felony in South Carolina?" Shelby asked.

"You're asking the wrong guy. I presume so. But Percy, check with Hortense and let's get our facts straight. Meanwhile, I'll get Chadwick moving."

"Will do, Mac," Percy responded.

After enjoying another drink, the three friends ended the ad hoc meeting. Percy headed home and Mac and Shelby went into Mac's house to scare up some sort of dinner or at very least, call for delivery.

"I think you finally have enough raw materials in the fridge and cabinets to yield a reasonable dinner," Shelby said. "Leave it to me this time."

"Suits me," Mac said. "Meanwhile, I'll call Chadwick."

The phone rang three times. Enough to make Mac worry just a bit.

"Hello", Chadwick said still being cautious.

"It's Mac."

"Thank goodness. I was wondering if you were going to call back."

"It hasn't been that long."

"Still."

"Okay. Here's what I want you to do. Do you have money?"

"I have credit cards,"

"No good. You can't use credit cards at all at this point, totally traceable. How much cash do you have?"

"I always carry a couple of hundred dollars."

"Okay, good. Here's what I want you to do. I want you to head for Atlanta. It's about a 9-hour drive from where you are now. I'll head that way, too. I'll text you a hotel where we can meet and plan next steps. I'll try to be there before you."

"Why do I have to go that far away? I'm confused."

"Because I think your hunch that your life is in danger is likely correct."

"If that's the case, then my wife is in danger, too."

"We'll look after her. But, first things first. Before they even know you aren't back in South Carolina, we need to move the chess pieces out of the way, if you catch my drift."

"How do I know you're not with them?"

"Come on. You called us … remember?"

"I suppose so."

"Then you'll be on your way?" Mac asked.

"I'll catch a couple of hours of sleep and get started, if that's okay," Nathan Chadwick suggested.

"I think that's fine."

"I'll probably drive straight through."

"Okay. I'll pick the hotel while you're sleeping and send you the text in short order," Mac assured him.

"Uh, Mr. Burns."

"Yes."

"Thank you."

Chapter 30

As Shelby continued with dinner, Mac fired up his old laptop and began looking for an appropriate hotel where he could meet with Chadwick safely. Shelby and Percy continued to pester Mac to buy a new laptop, but Mac had trouble justifying the investment given his retirement. Of course, thus far his retirement hadn't worked out quite as planned. Maybe he should consider a new Dell with all the bells and whistles. He supposed he would ask Shelby to help him shop in the next few days.

Mac found a Hilton Garden Inn on the Perimeter Highway.

"Shelby, do you want to go to Atlanta with me tomorrow?"

"I have a job, you know," Shelby scoffed.

"Surely you can get away for a couple of days. There is shopping to be accomplished," Mac knew how to sweeten the deal.

"And why would we need to go to Atlanta?"

"I need to meet with Chadwick and find out what he knows before involving the police," Mac explained.

"And at some point, I could do some shopping?" Shelby probed.

"Sure … after you sit in on the meeting."

"Figures."

"So, will you go?"

"I'll call the restaurant in the morning. Is three days enough?" Shelby asked.

"I think so."

Shelby sighed in resignation. In her mind, however, she did appreciate the fact that Mac wanted her to be involved in the "case". She knew Mac hated calling their involvement in these sort of investigations "cases", but that's what they seemed like to her. Mac often told her he respected her opinion and that was unique to her experience with men. Things could be worse, she figured.

Mac called the Hilton and made reservations. Even though Shelby pointed out that he could just as easily have made reservations online, he just didn't trust that method and wanted to talk to a human being. He booked two rooms. One in his name and one in the name of Justin Evans. He then texted Chadwick and identified the hotel, the location and told him to check in as Evans. Given that the room was prepaid, he hoped there would be no issue.

Mac and Shelby had a nice dinner of Salisbury steak and vegetables with baked potato and a glass of "house" chardonnay. House chardonnay in Mac's case was something called Cupcake—Grocery store selection to be certain, but not too bad.

After dinner, Mac's cell phone rang.

"Hello, Percy."

"Yep … it's definitely a felony. Hortense says it's full-on extortion and along the lines of kidnapping in terms of seriousness. So, these are bad dudes."

"Okay. I think I'm going to meet with Chadwick face to face tomorrow. I'll see what I can find out from him," Mac said.

"I'll be at the office if you need anything."

"Thanks, Percy. Goodnight."

"Goodnight, Mac."

Shelby was able to reach her manager the next morning and the couple left Bluffton around eleven. If traffic wasn't too bad, they should be at the Hilton in four to five hours. It was a beautifully sunny day Mac and Shelby enjoyed driving together. They also enjoyed visiting Atlanta together, although Mac's memories of the city were mixed. He'd been both a street cop and a detective there. He'd seen both the best of human nature and the worst during his career there, and ultimately was glad to get away to a less demanding environment.

By the time they got to the Perimeter, there was a major traffic jam. They had no idea the cause. Rush hour started a little early in Atlanta. Perhaps that was it or perhaps there was a pileup. No matter, Mac knew it would take them a good while to get to the hotel. As if it was planned, his phone rang.

"Mac Burns."

"Mr. Burns, it's me. Where are you?"

"Stuck in traffic. Where are you?"

"I'm in the hotel."

"Any problems?"

"No. No problems."

"Then just relax and we'll be there as soon as we can," Mac said.

"We?" Chadwick sounded nervous.

"Nothing to worry about. It's just my partner, Shelby Crewe."

"Uh … okay."

"Relax. All is well," Mac said, terminating the call.

"Partner?" Shelby said chuckling.

"I had to think about that for a moment," Mac admitted, "I almost said lady friend. Which would you have preferred?"

"Hmmm. Not sure. I guess partner is okay … serves the purpose either way," Shelby said.

It was another two hours before Max and Shelby reached the hotel. They checked in and settled into their room before ringing Chadwick's room. That is to say Justin Evan's room. They agreed to meet in the lobby for an initial discussion. Mac didn't think there was much chance there was any jeopardy in that decision. Neither he nor Chadwick would have reason to have been followed and they were hundreds of miles from Bartholomew's field of operations.

When Mac met Chadwick, he was rather surprised. The man was in fact rather robust looking. Over six feet tall, he supposed, with a shock of salt and pepper hair. He made him at over fifty years old, but not yet sixty. He was dressed in blazer and slacks, but no tie. He definitely didn't present as the timid man on the run that he sounded like on the phone.

"Hello, Mr. Evans," Mac stuck out his hand, using an abundance of caution.

"Mr. Burns, it's my pleasure," Chadwick responded.

"I'd like to present my partner, Ms. Crewe."

"You can call me Shelby, Mr. Evans," Shelby said.

"And I'm … uh … Justin," Chadwick replied, faltering only for a moment.

And so, it went for the first few minutes of their initial encounter. Mac didn't expect to accomplish much that first evening except to get over their awkwardness and Chadwick's distrust. After they had had a drink and dinner, he felt those goals had been achieved, so he suggested they get a good night's sleep and meet in Chadwick's room at 10AM the next morning.

At the appointed time the next morning Mac and Shelby were at Chadwick's door and knocked lightly. No answer. They knocked again. Now Mac was worried.

He pulled out his cell phone and called Chadwick's number. Chadwick answered after two rings.

"Where the hell are you?"

"In the lobby getting more coffee pods," Chadwick admitted.

"Damnit … I thought something was wrong. Get up here," Mac said, clearly miffed.

"Sorry … on my way."

Mac looked at Shelby.

"The man is in the middle of a caffeine jones. Of all times."

"Don't look at me. I'm just your partner," Shelby teased.

Chapter 31

Over the next few hours Nathan Chadwick filled Mac and Shelby in on everything he knew about Harry Bartholomew and his plans to extort money from the Sawgrass Electric Co-op and others in the Lowcountry. He shared how Bartholomew had installed Carl Munson into the top IT position in Sawgrass, how Munson had used the position to recruit and use top technical resources to manipulate the grids, in order to create a demonstration of how the electrical systems could cripple huge segments of the population in several counties, if demands weren't met. Mac was, of course, well aware of the "demonstration".

Chadwick also shared that he could find no evidence that anyone by the name Harry Bartholomew and with the background claimed by the man he knew, had ever lived. Same with Carl Munson. Of course, Mac assumed Bartholomew was actually Porter, so that information came as no surprise.

Later on, Chadwick said he had met a third man who had been strangely silent at their initial meeting. He couldn't remember the man's name nor had he ever seen him again. But he had been introduced as one of the partners, he did remember that.

Chadwick was afraid that his disappearance had thrown a monkey wrench into the master plan. Bartholomew was a methodical man and hated disruptions. That much Chadwick was able to determine. Clearly Chadwick controlled many of the resources Bartholomew needed to pulled off the scam. So, if Chadwick bailed, it might mean Bartholomew was back to square one or worse.

"I'll need to talk to Hortense about how she wants to proceed legally, of course, but as an officer of the court, there's something nagging at me," Mac said.

"Officer of the court?" Chadwick said, ears perking up.

"I used to be a detective here in Atlanta. Again, nothing to worry about now. I'm retired. At this point, I'm, what you might call, a consultant to the law firm."

"So, go on, Mac," Shelby urged.

What occurs to me is that it's Mr. Chadwick's word against that of a man that may or may not even exist—this Bartholomew character. You see what I mean?" Mac asked.

"In other words, he's more or less a ghost. Mr. Chadwick has seen him, but few others have." Shelby caught on.

"But you said Ms. Mendendo saw him, didn't you?" Chadwick asked logically.

"Well, maybe, but if so, not by that name," Mac pointed out.

"How about people like the waiters at the restaurant at Palmetto Bluff where I first met him?" Chadwick asked. "Surely, they would remember him. I'll bet he was a big tipper."

"Speaking from experience, I never much cared about a person's name even if I noticed it. That is, unless they were a regular," Shelby pointed out.

"Plus, isn't there normally a huge turnover in that business?" Mac asked.

"There is," Shelby answered, "…it's really a problem. I'd be surprised if those same people are there."

"And you never know when a waiter is slipped a large bill to forget seeing someone. I used to hear about that a lot when I was on the job here in Atlanta," Mac said.

"So, it's not as simple as sending the gendarme to his home and arresting him, is it?" Shelby asked.

"No. We're going to need to draw him out in some fashion." Mac responded.

"What am I going to do in the meantime?" Chadwick asked.

"Go as deep underground as possible and take your lovely wife with you," Mac responded, "We'll need to get a message to her letting her know that folks we send to pick her up are coming from you."

"We're also going to need a hell of a cover story," Chadwick said.

"We'll leave that to you, sir," Mac said.

"Right," Chadwick sniffed.

Mac and Shelby returned to their room telling Chadwick they needed to do some planning and coordinate with Hortense. They agreed to meet around five in the lobby to again, have a drink and dinner. Mac was hoping they could then send Nathan Chadwick on his way and they could enjoy a little "couple time" before heading back to Bluffton.

Percy was in Hortense's office when Mac called from their room.

"So, how are things progressing?" Hortense asked into the speaker phone.

"Mr. Chadwick gave us a fairly complete overview of how the scheme was to work and who the key players are," Mac said.

"Is the scheme dead now?" Percy asked.

"Can't say for sure, but Chadwick thinks it's running on fumes without him in place," Mac responded.

"What are you going to do with Chadwick now?" Hortense asked, "Should we have him arrested for his own protection?"

"Frankly, I wouldn't do that right now. We need for him to trust us and keep talking. I think just helping him lay low is a better idea," Mac replied.

"Understood," Hortense agreed.

"I have to ask you, Hortense. Did Franklin Porter say anything that made you believe he was Harry Bartholomew?" Mac asked.

Hortense thought intensely for a moment.

"No, Mac, he simply said he was behind it all. For all I know, he's the big boss and the guy you talk about as Bartholomew works for him."

"This is all getting more and more perplexing, isn't it?" Percy observed.

"Yes, it is," Mac agreed.

Mac and Shelby concluded their visit with Chadwick over dinner. Mac advised the man to take up residence at a small hotel in the suburb of Lawrenceville. Mac had used the place before. It was off the beaten track and definitely not a tourist destination. That said it was clean and accommodating and there were many restaurants nearby.

"I guess I can do that," Chadwick sighed, resigned to lying low, "but please, try to convince my wife to join me. I want her safe."

"We'll take good care of her, Mr. Chadwick."

Chadwick looked less than convinced.

Chapter 32

When Harry Bartholomew first arrived in the Low-country, he hadn't planned on staying long. Just long enough to squeeze some money from the local business community and ruin one Hortense Mondendo. He didn't figure that would take too long. The business leaders would figure to be rubes and Hortense just wouldn't see it coming. His grudge not only hadn't faded over the years, it had grown and developed into a hate so strong he could taste the need for revenge. He often asked himself why that incident in college had burned his ass so badly. No matter, he figured. It had and that was that.

As with any entrepreneur, of course, he needed somewhere to live—a base of operations, as it were. And Harry didn't much believe in throwing away money, so he decided to buy a rather modest home in a quaint community called Palmetto Bluff. Now modest by Palmetto Bluff standards was still expensive. There were many homes in that particular community that ranged into the millions. But Harry was able to find a relatively small, understated cottage for seven hundred thousand dollars. He paid cash.

Harry Bartholomew hated shopping. He called a local furniture store and insisted that a sales representative visit him at home. The salesperson made several recommendations and was somewhat chagrined when the stock answer from the buyer was "whatever". The net result was a home furnished in a manner that looked very much like a furniture store. But Harry didn't care. If he needed to do business, he did it over dinner at the hotel. He rarely used his own kitchen. If he dined in by himself, he ordered in.

Occasionally, Harry would escape to Savannah or Jacksonville for an evening of companionship. He had his contacts. Sometimes they were under different names, but they were still there.

Other than when he was working on his "projects", life was simple.

Until the call.

"Carl, I need to see you right away," Bartholomew shouted into the phone. "Meet me at the bar at the hotel in twenty minutes."

Bartholomew seldom took into account where any if his associates might be at any given moment. He did know that Carl would realize Harry meant the speakeasy style bar at the Montage. Hushed tones were the norm there and Harry Bartholomew favored hushed tones.

By the time Carl arrived, Bartholomew had downed one Old Fashioned and ordered another. His nerves were clearly on edge.

"What's up, Harry?" Carl said, clearly concerned. He'd never seen Bartholomew looking so pale.

"I thought you said you were sure she was dead."

"Sir?"

Both men were whispering but Carl nonetheless looked around furtively. There were only six other people in the dimly lit bar and light jazz music was playing softly, but still he worried.

"I thought she was dead and gone."

"Yes, sir. In the river, as I told you."

"Clearly not, since she called me not an hour ago."

"Who called you?" Carl whispered.

"That Ruby person."

"No, sir. That can't be. She's gone."

"You blew it, Carl. She's still alive," Harry argued.

"I'm telling you, sir, that's not possible. What did this person say?"

"She said '*Hello, Harry, it's Ruby, I'm really looking forward to meeting you. We have a lot to talk about. Call you soon.*' Or something like that," Bartholomew said.

"It's somebody bullshitting you, Harry. She's gone."

"You're sure?" Harry said, looking deadly serious.

"Positive. I know dead when I see it," Carl assured him, his stomach nonetheless in a knot.

Bartholomew sat back in his seat.

"Then, maybe you're right. Maybe some damned bitch is trying to get to me. Won't work," Harry chuckled, although inside his uneasiness continued.

"Will you buy me a drink, boss?" Carl asked.

"You should never call me boss, Carl. We're partners, remember. But I'll buy you a drink, if you'll do me a favor," Bartholomew responded.

"Sure, Harry, anything."

"I want you to go back there and look for her. See if you can find the … uh … body."

"Harry, it was in the water. Might be anywhere."

"Just try. Maybe you'll get lucky."

Carl saw that Harry Bartholomew was serious and wouldn't take no for an answer, so he agreed and sat back to enjoy a drink with his clearly shaken "partner".

The next morning, as promised, Carl returned to the banks of the Savannah River where he and Nicholas had met to do Bartholomew's bidding. Nicholas was an occasionally used two-bit criminal who would do most anything for the right price. Carl thought this man was below Harry's standards, but he needed muscle on occasion and Nicholas provided that, if not a scintilla of brain power.

That day Carl noticed that Nicholas showed no emotion at executing the gruesome task of dumping the contents of the body bag. A goon at best. Carl couldn't help but think about the brazen nature by which Bartholomew had written off the girl's young life. Ruby Wilder had simply been a minor impediment to the completion of Bartholomew's "projects". Worse still, maybe she was only a *possible* impediment. Bartholomew was notorious for jumping to conclusions about people's motivations when it came to his ambitions. What a waste, Carl thought.

As for Nicholas, Carl knew that he would be deemed by Bartholomew to be a loose end before leaving the Lowcountry for good and eliminated likely in a way similar to the way Bartholomew had dictated for poor Ruby.

If you had to visit the banks of the Savannah, he had picked a nice day to do so. Sunny and quite warm. He took a deep breath of the Lowcountry air and gazed off across the river. Carl even managed to skip a stone for a short stretch. Looking around for good measure, he returned to his car.

Carl Munson called Harry to confirm his findings or lack thereof.

"Sorry, Harry, but like I told you, the Savannah feeds into the Atlantic. She's probably in the ocean by now.

That was my plan," Carl said, hoping to calm Harry's concerns.

"You're probably right. I'll probably never hear from the caller again, but it does make me wonder how she got my number."

"That is strange, Harry. Let me give that some thought.

Carl, in fact, gave it no thought.

Chapter 33

Back in Bluffton Mac sat with Percy discussing Percy's work life. Both men had a dry martini in hand. Martinis were a rare selection, as they agreed it seemed a bit of a snotty choice for two "regular guys", which they agreed they were. That brought on a hearty laugh.

"Now that you're back in a law office, Percy, how are you feeling about trying to practice again?" Mac asked.

"I must admit that the juices are flowing again. On the other hand, Hortense keeps some unholy hours sometimes. I do nine to five, sometimes less," Percy admitted.

"But don't you feel like your skills as a barrister are being wasted?" Mac asked.

"I do on occasion, I must admit."

"I think you owe it to yourself to find out what steps you need to go through to be reinstated to the bar," Mac advised.

"You're right. I'll start making some calls. I really have no idea where to start, but maybe Hortense does. I know she'll be willing to help."

"I agree."

Talk turned to Bartholomew.

"So how are we going to go about drawing him out?" Percy asked.

"Maybe create some sort of a diversion that gets his attention, that causes him to react personally," Mac opined.

"What in world would that be?"

"No clue."

"What if we just arrested this Carl guy on suspicion of something or other? Would that get his attention?" Percy asked.

"Maybe. Or maybe he is callous enough to just let the guy take the rap and disappear into the night."

"I don't know, Mac, I think it might be worth a try. We could always let him go for lack of evidence, but if we hold him for couple of days and Bartholomew gets wind of it, maybe something pops," Percy suggested.

"Okay. Let's run it by Hortense," Mac said.

Hortense readily agreed with the idea and set things in motion with the Bluffton police.

The very next day Carl was pulled in for questioning. To say he was surprised was an understatement. Still, he knew how to keep his cool and claimed he had no earthly idea what the authorities were talking about or who this Bartholomew character was. He did seem to show genuine concern for his missing boss, Nathan Chadwick, however, and offered up any help he could provide.

Nonetheless, it was determined that Mr. Munson should spend a night or two in the Bluffton jail just for good measure. Contrary to the norm and official protocol, his cell phone was taken from him and later disappeared, so he was unable to make any calls, over vociferous protests.

Carl wasn't about to divulge any information about Bartholomew or anything at all for that matter. Not that Mac had expected him to. After all, arresting him was just a diversion. That said, they had probable cause, so they were covered.

Bartholomew had tried to call Carl Munson several times and was growing frantic. What the hell could have happened to him?

The second call couldn't have come at a worse time for Bartholomew. This time a message was left when he didn't pick up.

"*Hi Harry! It's Ruby again. I just hate this time of year, don't you? Too chilly. Too damp for me. Listen to silly me. A northern girl complaining about the weather down here being cool and damp. Listen, Harry, let's plan on getting together in the next few days. I think we need to settle up. Don't you? Bye now!*"

Bartholomew picked up the message quickly, hoping it was Carl. After hearing it, he sat silently for several minutes trying to understand what he was hearing. It took some doing, but he convinced himself he was dealing with someone trying to make him lose his mind or take him for his money or some combination thereof.

But he would outsmart whomever it was. Now he had a third project. Get the bitch or the people who would be foolish enough to try to do this to him. How stupid could you get? How stupid, indeed.

Carl was finally released from the Bluffton jail and knew that the first thing he should do is call Harry. Instead, he headed to a little bar he knew in Old Town Bluffton and threw back two screwdrivers in record time. Now he was ready for the world. Or at least Harry Bartholomew.

He made the call.

"Where have you been, Carl? Where the fuck have you been?" Bartholomew demanded.

"Well, Harry, to be frank, I've been in jail. That's where the fuck I've been," Carl took a chance mocking his boss.

"Jail? Why?"

"Well for starters they think I have something to do with a little thing called extortion. Something also to do with power outages. All news to me boss," Carl said again mockingly.

"You said nothing?"

"What do you think, Harry?"

"Sorry, Carl, I know you wouldn't talk. I'm just a little spooked right now."

"Another message?"

"Yes, but I realize it's a shakedown. I'm not biting."

"Good. I'll get on it. We'll find them and maybe they'll end up in the river, too," Carl said.

"I appreciate that, Carl, but let's take this a step at a time. Why don't we meet for a nice dinner tonight? No agenda. Just a nice dinner at the hotel."

"You're on, Harry," accepting the gesture for what it was.

Harry needed a friend.

Chapter 34

Hortense hadn't given Porter much thought recently until Mac asked the question about the connection to Bartholomew. Now she wondered if she missed something. Something that could help them bring some really bad people down. Her own suppressed emotions the day he visited her office might have caused her to overlook a comment or inference. She hated that. As an attorney, she was trained not to let that happen. In fact, much like a poker player, she knew to watch for "tells". But she recalled none from that day.

Hortense rang Percy in his office.

"Percy."

"Has there been any reaction from Bartholomew?" Hortense asked.

"None that we've tracked, Hortense, but frankly, I'm not exactly sure what we'd be looking for."

"Point taken. It's not like he'd make a frantic call to the police," Hortense admitted. "I rather thought it might be more like a threatening call about the grid."

"Nothing there, either," Percy responded, "And when you think of it, with Chadwick and his boy Carl at least temporarily sidelined, his toolkit was getting pretty bare."

"Right. Well let's give it some more time. Meanwhile see what Mac wants to do and we can talk about it tomorrow," Hortense suggested. "I'm heading home a little early today."

Porter was waiting for her in the parking lot. Hortense wasn't prepared for that. He was sitting in a non-descript car. Nothing flashy. Probably a rental. No doubt rented under an alias, she figured.

Porter made no move to exit the car. He rolled down his window. Hortense winced thinking he was about to pull a weapon, but no such thing happened

"Hortense," Porter said, "be careful not to get ahead of yourself. Back in school, you thought you were smarter than me, but that wasn't true then, and it isn't true now. Just be careful. I'm bound to win this round."

Then Porter pulled away without another word.

Hortense was sufficiently shaken that she quickly returned to her office and told Percy what had just happened. Percy then called Mac and brought him up to date.

"Let me talk to Hortense, please, Percy," Mac said.

"Sure, Mac."

"Hortense, I'm so sorry this happened," Mac said into the phone.

"Scared me to death, Mac, I have to admit. I thought he was going to shoot me," Hortense admitted.

"I have to ask you the same question I asked you before. Did he say or do anything that might link him to Bartholomew?"

"No, Mac, and this time I was even more sensitized to it. He's being really careful with his words, I can tell."

"Okay, Hortense, thank you. We'll figure all of this out, I assure you." Mac tried to make the attorney feel better.

Hortense handed the phone back to Percy.

"Do you think we're dealing with the same man, Mac?"

"I do, Percy, but he's doing a good job of hiding that fact. I hope I'm right. Otherwise, our troubles are twofold."

"What's next?" Percy asked.

"I think we should take a ride out to Palmetto Bluff and sniff around a bit. Chadwick said he had a meeting or two out there. Maybe someone, a waiter or waitress remembers Bartholomew, even though Shelby thinks it's a longshot."

"Maybe she should tag along, since she can speak their language," Percy suggested.

"Good idea. I'll ask her."

Later between the lunch and dinner hours they piled into Mac's truck and headed west toward Palmetto Bluff.

"I still say, you can't expect to find out much," Shelby said, repeating her earlier misgiving.

"I understand, Shelby, but it can't hurt to ask around," Mac countered.

The results of questioning the wait staff at the eateries and bars were something more than blank stares. The looks were more like worried, eyes averted, looks that betrayed concern. No amount of reassuring could pry information from even one of the service people. Finally, a food service manager appeared.

"Who are you and what is your business here?" the man said in a calm, but authoritative voice.

"I'm Detective Mac Burns and these are my colleagues Richard Percival from the Martin, Speckman and Mendendo law firm in Beaufort. Ms. Shelby Crewe is a consultant. We're looking for one Harry Bartholomew," Mac ad-libbed.

"I have no knowledge of the man you seek, Detective Burns. By the way, what jurisdiction do you serve?"

"What is your name, sir?" Mac countered.

"I'm Mr. Pilkerton."

"Mr. Pilkerton, I'm from Atlanta working in conjunction with the Bluffton police department, as is Mr. Percival," Mac said managing to skirt the question.

"Well, Detective Burns from Atlanta, I'm afraid we can be of no assistance, so if your business is complete, I would appreciate your moving along before you upset my staff any further."

"I was unaware we were upsetting your staff, Mr. Pilkerton."

"Wasn't it obvious?"

"No, sir. And that wasn't our mission. Should we speak to them before we leave? I hate leaving them with bad feelings about our visit," Mac knew the answer to expect.

"I would appreciate it very much if you would not do that, sir," Pilkerton said putting his hand on Mac's shoulder, as if to encourage him out the door.

As they re-entered Mac's truck, Percy stated the obvious.

"Those are some spooked people."

"But I have to wonder what has them spooked," Shelby said.

"Could be as simple as Pilkerton telling them to keep their mouth shut about patrons," Mac opined.

"True," Shelby said, "I've known some people who have worked out there and it's a stiff environment, catering to people who are well off. You'd be wise to just be quiet about what you see or hear around the restaurants and the managers, I'm sure, remind them of that."

"Or it could also be that Bartholomew has a reputation of being dangerous," Percy reminded them.

"Or a combination of the two," Mac said.

The drove in silence for a few minutes.

"We're missing something, aren't we?" Percy said."

"It's obvious, isn't it?" Mac agreed.

"But what?" Shelby asked, not fully understanding.

"There's no clear thread holding all of this mess together. Nathan doesn't know much, Carl may not be fully up to date, the people at Palmetto Bluff may just be afraid of their shadow, and Hortense is in the dark. No one has a clue what's in that dark closet either by design or by omission," Mac explained.

"Is that Bartholomew's doing?" Percy wondered.

"I think maybe he figured he would collect the money from the co-ops before he ever had to actually connect the dots for all the players. Keep everyone guessing, scoop up the money and move on. Not a bad plan, actually," Mac explained. "Meanwhile, no one even knows if you exist."

"But now he's just flailing around, isn't he?" Shelby asked.

"Presumably," Mac responded, "and it must be driving him crazy. But it's like a wounded animal. It makes them more dangerous than ever."

When they got back to Old Town, Shelby went off to her own dinner service. Mac and Percy decided to forego their normal afternoon cocktail and walk down to the May River for a little exercise.

"Mac, I'm worried about Hortense," Percy admitted, "I think this Porter thing has her off her game."

"Maybe we need to focus on him for now and hope that leads to Bartholomew. That might help Hortense relax a bit," Mac suggested.

"I think that's a good idea," Percy agreed.

Chapter 35

Since Hortense had described the car as what looked like a typical rental, the two men decided to start by checking with the local auto rental companies the next morning. Several phone calls and two visits later, they found an Enterprise location that had rented a midsize sedan to one F. Porter. Had Hortense's tormentor made a mistake?

Mac took no time in visiting the Enterprise office to see if the rental agent could remember the man who rented the car. Not much luck there. However, at that particular location, the renter was required to leave an imprint of his or her driver's license. Trouble was, by what authority would Mac ask to see or better still, get a copy of that document?

"I'm Detective Mac Burns working with the Bluffton Police Department," Mac said, showing his Atlanta badge just briefly. "I need to see your records for a rental by a man named Porter on last Wednesday. It's important. Police business."

The clerk didn't hesitate to pull the file and hand it to Mac. Sloppy work, Mac thought, but he appreciated a little sloppiness when it benefited him. There was a picture of the man's driver's license included in the file. It showed a man in what appeared to be in his fifties, salt and pepper hair, no smile, no facial hair, utterly unremarkable face.

"I need a copy of this," Mac said sounding as detective like as possible.

The clerk ran a copy of the entire file, about three pages. One page included the renter's local address, in this case a hotel on route 278. Doubtful he was still there, since the car had been returned, but worth checking.

Mac thanked the clerk and returned to his truck. He spent a minute looking at the driver's license. The address shown was in Baltimore, Maryland. Mac knew the license could be a fake, of course. Anyone could buy one for a hundred dollars or less. But at least they might have a picture of Porter, if not Bartholomew.

Deciding to head over to the Hampton Inn mentioned in the rental paperwork, Mac called Shelby to give her an update, but got no answer. He arrived at the hotel in just a few minutes and entered the small lobby.

He saw no one on duty and no one waiting to check in.

"Hello?" Mac said.

"Oh, sorry …" a young woman said, emerging from the back room, "Just catching up on some paperwork."

Mac wondered what kind of paperwork a desk clerk at a chain hotel might be responsible for.

"No problem. I'm looking for Mr. Porter. I was supposed to meet him here," Mac said with faint hope.

"Mr. Porter?" the woman said addressing the computer terminal.

"Yes, Ma'am, Franklin Porter. He said he was going to stay here while in town. He's an old friend. Can you help me?" Mac adlibbed.

"I see an F. Porter in room 213, but he checked out about 45 minutes ago. Looks like you just missed him, sir," the clerk said apologetically.

"What a shame, we were supposed to have lunch."

"You might check One Hot Mamas over on 278. Mr. Porter asked for a lunch recommendation and that's the place that came to mind. Great barbeque, wings … that sort of thing. He might be there," the young clerk offered up.

"Thanks very much," Mac said, "I'll try there."

Mac made his way over to Buckwalter Place and route 278 and entered One Hot Mamas with low expectations. After explaining to the greeter that he was looking for his lunch companion he began scanning the room for Porter or Bartholomew or whomever. Finally, he saw a man sitting alone at a table slowing eating a salad and looking contemplative. He sat down without asking permission.

"Gee, Mr. Bartholomew, it seems odd to see someone eating a salad at a barbeque joint. What's the story?"

"You obviously have me confused with someone else, sir. Please leave my table."

"No, I think you are either Harry Bartholomew or Franklin Porter or perhaps both. What say you?"

"I say leave my table immediately or I will call the authorities," the man responded.

"Turns out, I am the authorities," Mac lied yet again.

"Oh … then show me your badge … not that it would matter since I am neither of those people."

Mac flashed his badge quickly hoping that's all it would take. It didn't.

"I'm a quick study, sir. That was a badge from Atlanta. You have no authority here. Now please leave my table before I call local the local authorities."

Knowing that pursuing the discussion further would be fruitless at this point, Mac stood up.

"Mr. Porter, I'm fairly certain of who you are and what you've done. I suggest you cease and desist. Please take note. My name is Mac Burns and I can be your worst enemy if you don't, I assure you."

"Noted, although you are totally incorrect about who I am. Have a nice day sir," The man said, a little too dismissively.

Mac left the restaurant convinced that he had encountered Franklin Porter, if not Bartholomew. He decided to wait in the parking lot and follow the man when he had finished his lunch.

When the man Mac thought was Porter left One Hot Mamas, he entered a Mercedes sedan. Mac wasn't surprised, given who he thought the man might be. Mac managed to follow the Mercedes further up highway 278 towards Interstate 95. He lost the car near the partially hidden entrance to the road to Palmetto Bluff. That didn't mean the man had turned into that road, but it was consistent with Mac's suspicions. Mac broke off the tail at that point.

The man at the restaurant had failed to notice that Mac had managed to snap a picture of him with his iPhone. His intent was to head to Beaufort to show the picture to Hortense to determine if the man was, in fact, Porter.

Forty minutes later Mac was sitting in Hortense's office with Percy showing the two of them the picture.

"Yes, Mac, that's Franklin Porter," Hortense affirmed, "I'm surprised he allowed himself to be found. But yes, that's him."

"That's one step forward, but we still have to link him with Bartholomew," Mac pointed out.

"That's the tough part," Percy said. "That's definitely the challenge."

Chapter 36

Harry Bartholomew was getting to the point that he was skittish about answering his phone. The calls from "Ruby", phony or not, were unsettling. Neither he nor Carl had been able to determine the source of the calls and that was unusual. Harry's influence was deep and wide and his contacts solid. Normally, he could simply ask and information would flow his way. Not this time. This time there was roaring silence. Worrisome. Very worrisome.

As if preordained, the phone did ring and the voice of Ruby was on the other end.

"Hi Harry. Gosh I've been meaning to call you. I'm over at the hotel right now. Want to come over and meet me for a drink. Want me to come over to your place? Your choice. Harry? Harry??"

Bartholomew felt as if he had to answer.

"I'll come to the hotel and meet you. Should I bring money?"

"Oh, my, no, Harry, this isn't about money. I just want you to look me in the face and tell me why … ya know? After that we can settle up. See you in a bit."

The call ended.

Harry Bartholomew had no intention of going to the hotel then or ever again. Harry called Carl.

"Yes, Harry," Carl answered, slightly slurring from one too many cocktails.

"I want you to go to the hotel to see if you see anyone that might be making the calls," Bartholomew virtually commanded.

"Now?" Carl wanted to know. "Why now?"

"I got another call and she wanted to meet up there. I'm not going there myself, but whoever it is, won't be expecting you."

"Okay, okay. I'll take a look around, but I don't expect much," Carl said, sounding disgusted.

"Careful, Carl, you still work for me," Bartholomew reminded him.

"Oh, hell yes, don't I know."

An hour later Carl knocked on Harry's door. Harry carefully peered through the peephole and then opened the door to his right-hand man.

"Harry, it's mostly couples up there and a few businessmen and golfers. No single women, no one even resembling Ruby in the least, and trust me I would know."

"I'm not surprised but I had to know."

"I'm going home to bed, if you don't mind," Carl said.

"Sure, Carl, and thanks."

Bartholomew made sure to check all the locks on the doors in his house and sat down to read before turning in.

Almost as if expected, the phone rang again. Bartholomew knew he had to answer.

"Pretty chicken shit, Harry. I thought you would show up, but I should have known better. Your boy couldn't find his butt with both hands. Next time, I'll just have to come to you, that's all. Have a good night!"

Bartholomew was more than stunned. Whoever was harassing him had seen Carl and knew that he had been sent by Harry. Harry Bartholomew realized he had totally lost control of his environment and the projects he had started in South Carolina.

He had never been compromised to this degree. He didn't know who he could trust or what he could believe. He wasn't even certain he could get a good night's sleep.

In another sequestered location, Nathan Chadwick felt abandoned. He had heard nothing further from Mac Burns and nothing from his wife. What the hell was going on? Did he venture a call to either of them and risk giving away his location? The hotel they put him in was adequate, but remote. He had naturally assumed he would be joined by his wife, as he awaited further instructions and perhaps even more protection.

Chadwick decided to call Mac Burns. He figured the detective would take measures to ensure calls from him were not traced, although he couldn't imagine how.

"Mac Burns."

"Mr. Burns … what the hell is going on?"

Mac knew immediately who was calling by the ID on the burner phone, so he didn't mention Chadwick's name.

"Arrangements are being made, sir, but it takes time. Are you getting what you need in the meantime?"

"Within reason, I suppose."

"Just be patient for a little while longer. You are safe and so is your significant other."

"So, when will my 'other' be joining me?" Chadwick asked sarcastically.

"Within the week. It took some convincing, as we expected," Mac responded.

"Alright. I'll be here," Chadwick stated the obvious.

Mac knew Nathan Chadwick was growing impatient and that could end up being a problem. They needed his testimony to bring down Bartholomew and his crew, so getting the co-op president his wife was of growing importance. He called Percy and asked that the plan to do that very thing be hurried up.

Because Porter had headed in the general direction of Palmetto Bluff, Mac decided to venture over there again to see if he could turn up anything on a resident named Porter. He gained entrance by claiming to be heading to the hotel. Once in he began driving around the neighborhoods looking for names on mailboxes. No luck there. He decided to stop by the real estate office and see if he could find out any more about Porter.

"Yes, sir," a reception person said as Mac entered. "Are you looking to buy in Palmetto Bluff?"

Mac couldn't help but notice that the reception person looked at him as if he was from another planet, perhaps because of his attire. This particular day Mac had dressed in fatigue pants and a chambray shirt. Hardly the Palmetto Bluff mode of dress.

"No. I'm just looking for an old college friend, Franklin Porter. I'm told he bought a home here. Can you help me?"

"We really can't provide information about our owners, sir," the rather stiff receptionist replied.

"I'm sorry to hear that. I've driven hundreds of miles for our reunion. I hate to miss it."

"Reunion?"

"Yes. Harvard Law, in fact," Mac decided on a whopper.

"I see," the receptionist said changing attitude and clearly impressed. "Let me see what I can do for you."

The clerk accessed what Mac assumed was a database file on her computer and shortly came back with the answer he was looking for.

"I see that an F. Porter bought a home just six months ago, in fact. Do you think that might be your friend?"

"I'd be willing to bet, it is," Mac responded.

The clerk gave Mac the address and directions without further hesitation and Mac left thanking her profusely.

Mac immediately drove to that address and parked a block or so away from the immediate sightline. He thought he would just wait for a while and see if Porter emerged from the home. No such luck. However, now that he had the address, he knew they could stake out the location at any time and decided to head back to Old Town for the moment.

Things were finally coming together.

Chapter 37

Now that Mac and Percy felt they had a lead on Porter and might be able to pull him in when needed, they decided to concentrate on Bartholomew. Percy suggested it was time to show Carl and Chadwick the picture of Porter to finally establish the link, and then formally depose them about Bartholomew's criminal endeavors before arresting him. In fact, maybe drawing him out wouldn't be necessary. Maybe they found a way to link him to Porter and that in itself would do the trick.

The remaining challenge might be charging him for anything beyond attempted extortion. Murder was tough to prove without a body. No one had even reported Ruby Wilder missing. For all anyone knew, she could have returned to New England and the life she lived before.

The two men were in Percy's office at the law firm planning next steps when the phone rang.

"Percival. Okay … great … thanks."

"What's up?" Mac asked.

"Chadwick's wife has joined him."

"Thank goodness."

"So, what now?" Percy asked.

"I think we need to have a long talk with Carl Munson," Mac responded.

"You going to have the Bluffton PD pull him in?" Percy asked.

"No, I think we'll take a less formal approach and just call him ourselves. I suspect he'll speak with us."

"Hope so."

Mac had retained Carl's phone number and called him right away.

"Mr. Munson, Mac Burns here. You remember me?"

"Hell, yes, I remember you. Cost me a couple of good days of my life, as I recall," Carl replied.

"No, sir, that was all about you and Mr. Bartholomew. Anyway, I'm just calling to offer to buy you lunch. You free tomorrow?"

"You must be kidding. Why would I have lunch with you, Burns?"

"Because it beats the hell out of the Bluffton jail for one."

"Point taken, I guess. Where? What time?"

"Let's meet at Captain Woody's at 12:30, shall we?"

"Sure … and you're buying right?"

"As I said."

"Okay. I'll be there."

The next day Mac and Percy met Carl Munson at the popular Bluffton restaurant at the appointed time. Carl had continued to execute his duties at Sawgrass Electric Co-op, so he was dressed in a blue blazer, grey slacks, open white-collar button-down shirt and tasseled loafers. He looked anything but the serial criminal Mac supposed him to be.

The men ordered lunch and Mac got right to the point.

"Carl, I have to ask. What do you know about the death of Ruby Wilder?"

"Look. Ruby is or was a girl who worked at the co-op. I only met her once. As far as I know, she's alive and well."

"So, you had nothing to do with her death?" Mac pressed.

"Mr. Burns, I'm an information systems guy. I love animals, keep plants and wouldn't hurt a flea. Ask anyone."

The food came quickly and the three men began eating.

"I really only have one other thing to go over with you, Mr. Munson," Mac said pulling out the copy of the driver's license of Franklin Porter.

"Do you recognize this man?" Mac said holding the paper in front of Carl Munson

Carl looked frozen for a moment and then seemed to snap out of it.

"Naw. Can't say I've ever seen him. Why?"

"Because we think this Porter guy is also Harry Bartholomew … your boss," Mac said.

"My boss is Nathan Chadwick," Carl countered.

Percy chuckled.

"What's so funny?" Carl said, seeming perturbed.

"Well, Mr. Chadwick seems to be on the run from your other boss, Mr. Bartholomew. I gather he's a dangerous man. Is that right?"

"I don't know a Bartholomew, so I can't say. Now, if we're finished here, I'll get back to my job," Carl tried to wrap things up.

"Here's a news release for you, Carl. We'll soon be arresting Franklin Porter, and we think Bartholomew will be caught up in that and he'll be taking people down with him. You might want to get ahead of that. Just giving you fair warning."

"Thanks. Don't know Porter. Don't know Bartholomew. Bye."

With that, Carl Munson exited the restaurant without another word.

"Well, Percy, Mr. Munson seems to be a man of pretty strong resolution. He's either extremely loyal to Bartholomew or has his own agenda. Hard to tell."

"I'm assuming you aren't considering that he could be innocent?" Percy asked.

"Not for even a minute," Mac responded.

Percy realized that was entirely based on Mac's cop instincts and respected that. It had paid off many times.

Driving back to the co-op, Carl Munson called Harry Bartholomew.

"Hello, Carl."

"Harry, this Burns guy just told me they are about to arrest a man named Franklin Porter, who looks a hell of a lot like you. Just thought I'd tell you."

"Well, thanks, Carl. Has nothing to do with me, but I appreciate you letting me know." Bartholomew played it as cool as he was capable.

Bartholomew found himself wringing his hands and considering the implications of the arrest of Porter. How and where would they do it? He couldn't fathom it. He began to retrace every step of his existence for the past several days. Normally, he was confident that he made no mistakes just as he demanded that his people make no mistakes. But somewhere along the line, he had dropped the ball this time. Now he had to consider moving on without the payoff he had hoped for. What a shame. What a shame, indeed.

Chapter 38

Mac's cell phone rang and he recognized Shelby's number immediately.

"Hey girl! What's up?"

"Well, I'll tell you, sir. I'm in the mood for a little male companionship and I think you're just the man for the job," Shelby said.

"I'm awfully glad to hear that. Are you on your way here?" Mac asked.

"I just want to stop off at my place to freshen up and I'll be right there." Shelby replied, "But let's go out for dinner, okay?"

"Sure, whatever you want, and wherever you want."

"Be there if a jiff, hon."

With a few minutes to spare, Mac took the opportunity to freshen up himself. He had no idea where Shelby might want to go for dinner but unlike himself, she tended to want to head over to the island on their frequent date nights. He fought it at first because of all the tourists, but realized that he usually lost the battle and anyway, loved her enough to give in on that one small point.

Shelby arrived in about thirty minutes and suggested that they go to a restaurant on the island called Cowboy. Mac admitted he'd never heard of it and wasn't sure he was interested. But when Shelby explained that they specialized in lots and lots of meat, Mac softened considerably.

Mac was pleasantly surprised when the waiter explained how the restaurant served the tables. After getting salads and sides at a buffet, meats just kept coming until, as Mac called it, you hollered "uncle". Actually, you had to turn over a small coaster like card from the green side to the red side to stop service and indicate that you'd had enough.

As they sat enjoying a cocktail Mac brought Shelby up to date on the situation with the extortion attempt at the co-ops. Shelby was surprised at how far along the case had progressed.

Mac noticed that Shelby looked troubled.

"What's on your mind, lady?" Mac asked.

"It's that girl … Ruby. I can't help but remember that call. I know she was reaching out for help and I was not in a position to help her then."

"Even now we don't know what's become of her. She may be okay and back home in New England," Mac said, trying his best to reassure Shelby.

"Well, when you know something definitively, I want you to be straight with me. Even if it's bad news. Okay?"

"Of course, Shelby. I don't hold things back from you. Ever."

Mac had noticed that Shelby had somehow identified with Ruby Wilder ever since they had asked her to deliver the message to the young mistress at the Nectar bar. Shelby had pegged the young woman as a victim and felt as if the investigation was tightening the grip on her no matter how righteous. He hoped Shelby hadn't reached out to Ruby Wilder on her own.

After dinner Mac and Shelby returned to Mac's house, enjoying an evening of binge watching a Netflix series they'd been meaning to watch, sipping on Prosecco and following up with a little active cuddling.

The next morning Shelby had an announcement to make. Over scrambled eggs and sausage she let Mac know that she had been offered the general manager position at the fish house. Not a shift management position, but general manager. She had been blindsided by the offer. It meant considerably more salary, of course, more responsibility, but potentially more hours.

Mac sat silently for a moment.

"Congratulations, Shelby! I couldn't be prouder of you!"

"Thanks, Mac. But what do you think I should do?"

"What do you mean? What do you want to do?"

"I want to do what's best for us," Shelby responded.

"Shelby, I'm not going to advise you on this. I want you to do what you feel is right for you and I'll support you no matter what."

"We have trouble making time work out already, Mac. I don't want more constraints."

"If you want this job, we'll make it work."

"I don't know that I do."

"Only you can determine that," Mac pointed out.

The couple decided to drop the subject and pick it up later. Mac wasn't sure which way Shelby was leaning in terms of the job. Nor was he sure which way he was leaning in terms of how he wanted her to decide. No, he was lying to himself. He didn't want her to take it. In fact, he wanted her to be with him all the time, but he knew she wanted a certain amount of independence.

So, he would simply continue to profess his support and offer any advice that didn't push her one way or another … but only if she asked.

By late morning, Shelby was preparing to head to the restaurant for the lunch shift. She was brushing her hair facing the mirror on the chest of drawers in his bedroom.

"Shelby, before you go, I have to ask you a question," Mac said.

"About the job offer?" Shelby said, not turning towards him.

"No. Couldn't be further from that subject and I know you may think I'm crazy."

"I already think that, so spit it out," Shelby said turning around and looking quizzically in Mac's direction.

"Have you had any contact with Ruby since you met her at the Nectar bar?"

Shelby looked completely taken aback. She was silent for many seconds.

"Mac, don't you think I would have told you if I had? I know how important that sort of thing is to you."

"I would have thought so, but I also know you felt sorry for her and the apparent mess she got herself into."

"Not so much that I would meddle. No, Mac, no contact at all. I'm hoping she isn't, but based on what you're telling me, I assume she's dead," Shelby said, turning back around.

"Thanks, Shelby. Sorry to have asked," Mac said, leaving the bedroom. As he did, he thought he heard gentle sounds of crying.

Chapter 39

"I think I really blew it with Shelby this morning, Percy," Mac said as he sipped his Bombay and Tonic.

The two men were relaxing on Mac's front porch after Percy returned from the office, as was their practice. The little terrier, Hero, was lying at Mac's feet, as was **his** practice.

"What did you do this time, pray tell?" Percy asked.

"For some reason, I asked her if she had had any contact with Ruby Wilder since we sent her to speak with the girl at the Nectar bar."

"What in the world would make you think she might have?"

"You remember she got what she thought was a call from Ruby. The girl didn't say anything but Shelby surmised that Ruby was in trouble. That's why she wanted us to check on her," Mac explained. "I just think she never stopped worrying about her."

"Still, Shelby doesn't strike me as the kind of person who would take matters into her own hands and try to find Ruby," Percy pointed out.

"I know and me asking her made her feel like I just didn't trust her. That was a first in our relationship."

"What do you think will happen next?"

"I'll pay a price for sure. I hope it's only the silent treatment but … man … it could be worse."

"Well, if you don't mind me saying so, you kind of deserve it," Percy said.

"I wish I didn't agree with you, but I do," Mac admitted.

Mac and Percy sat for a few minutes pondering Mac's immediate future before readdressing the other challenges at hand.

"So, are we going to stake out the Porter house at Palmetto Bluff, and if so, who would we get to do it?"

"Stake out? Now you're using TV cop jargon? Well, the answer is—we should. As to the second question, I have no idea. Neither you, nor I, can do it," Mac responded, mocking Percy only slightly.

"How about Kevin?" Percy suggested. "He's on a break from school right now and looking to make a little money. Maybe the law firm could front him a few dollars to watch the house for a few hours each day."

Kevin was a young man living in Percy's home. Mac had encountered him trying to hold up a gas station at a Walmart, but the two men, in conjunction with the Bluffton Police, had managed to set him on the right path. He was now in college and doing well. Technically, Hero was his dog, but Mac ended up taking care of the pup most days when he was home.

"Sure, Percy, see what you can make happen," Mac agreed.

Mac had tried calling Shelby after he knew lunch service had ended and later about six in the evening. No answer, no return call. He contemplated driving over to Shelby's condo, or villa as they called them in the Lowcountry, but thought better of it. That trust thing again.

Mac ended up going to bed early still worried about Shelby. About midnight his cell phone rang.

"Mac," he answered trying to sound alert.

"Don't do that to me again, Mac. I mean it," Shelby said. "Understood."

"Goodnight. See you tomorrow for breakfast," Shelby said her voice softening.

Mac slept a little better from that point on … but only a little better.

When Shelby came by for breakfast the next morning, no mention was made of the Ruby question. They did read-dress Shelby's job offer though.

"I'm not going to take the offer, Mac," Shelby said over scrambled eggs and bacon.

"That seemed pretty definitive. Why so?" Mac asked, almost timidly.

"Two reasons. I don't want to take any more time from us and second, I want to go back to school."

"But won't that also take time away from us?"

"Much of it I can do from home on my computer and at my own speed. I've done the investigation and I think I can make it work for us," Shelby responded, almost enthusiastically.

"Well, if your mind is made up, I'm totally on board. Should we revisit living together again in that case?" Mac tested the waters.

"Too much, too soon," Shelby said, smiling slightly.

"Got it," Mac said, understanding her response.

Mac was happy to learn that Shelby didn't have a shift that day and they could relax together, maybe take a drive. He decided to call Percy and sign off for the day. Bar-tholomew could wait he figured.

"That's fine, Mac. That said, I got the law firm to agree to pay Kevin to keep an eye on the Porter home for four to six hours a day. Hortense even managed to get him a gate pass somehow. I didn't ask questions."

"And he'll report back to you then?"

"Yes, checking in every couple of hours."

"Great. I'll have my cell phone on me, but don't call unless absolutely necessary. We're working though some things. Ya know?"

"Been there, Mac."

Mac and Shelby decided to drive down to Savannah for lunch. Shelby loved the Charthouse on the riverfront. Settling in for lunch, the couple resorted to small talk, so that things that might cause conflict were well behind them. They decided that after lunch they would play tourists and jump on a trolley tour to visit the historic districts around Savannah. As long as they had lived in the area, neither of them had taken advantage of that sort of attraction. Both Mac and Shelby relaxed and enjoyed the diversion. Life seemed back to a semblance of normal.

Chapter 40

Kevin had been watching the home in Palmetto Bluff for several days now and was rather surprised at the lack of comings and goings. He figured people usually had to at least head out to the grocery store or the pharmacy, but no one had emerged from the house in all the time he had been assigned to the property. Of course, he was only there for a certain number of hours each day, staggered as they might be. Maybe the grocery shopping hours were equally staggered. Anyway, this 'stake out', as Percy called it. turned out to be pretty boring. Nonetheless Mac and Percy were paying him well. In fact, they had always been good to him, ever since he had been stupid enough to try to rob a gas station.

Suddenly, there was a rap on the driver's side window. A man in uniform beckoned him out of the car.

"What are you doing here?" the man asked.

"And who's asking?" Kevin responded, taking no small chance.

"I'm with the Palmetto Bluff Security Force," the man responded, pointing to a sort of badge on his chest.

"Force? That's an intimidating word," Kevin said, still pushing his luck. "Do you intend to use force?"

"What … what are you saying?"

"Look, I'm here working with the Bluffton Police surveilling a home legally. Shall I call the precinct?"

"No, no … just show me your badge," the man responded.

"I have no badge, sir, I'm a private contractor. I'll just call the precinct."

Kevin put his cell phone on speaker and called Mac.

"Officer Burns," Mac said, having prepared for such an eventuality.

"Officer Burns, I'm being detained by … let's see, what was your name, sir?"

"Never mind my name … go on with your work," the man said, heading back to his car.

"Thank you, Officer Burns," Kevin said.

Kevin went on with his work. It was just after that time that he noticed a man loading some bags into a Mercedes parked in the driveway of the house he was watching. Using binoculars, he saw that they looked more like duffle bags than suitcases.

A short time later, Bartholomew found himself sitting in his sparsely furnished bedroom contemplating going on the run. He hated that phrase and even the thought of what it meant. He'd never done that. He'd simply become someone else and used the money he had managed to gain from one project or another to set himself up in another location. He made certain his credentials were impeccable in each case.

He thumbed through a number of identifications he always had at hand. Who would he become this time and where would he go? He realized he had to make a move quickly, so he picked up the suitcase he kept packed for such an occasion and headed for the Mercedes parked in front of his house. The rest of all that mattered to the current Harry Bartholomew was already in the vehicle. He pulled from the driveway and headed for the exit of Palmetto Bluff for what he supposed would be forever. Goodbye to the Low-country, goodbye to South Carolina and goodbye to Harry Bartholomew. He could only hope that also meant goodbye to Ruby Wilder.

Kevin knew he had to call Mac when he saw the man leave the house he was watching. He also knew he had to follow, at least for a while.

"Officer Bu—," Mac was unable to complete his greeting.

"Mac, he's on the move. I'm following him for now, but his car is loaded—suitcases and all," Kevin said breathlessly.

"Well, stay with him while you can and let's stay connected, so you can tell me if he's headed to the interstate or in another direction."

In short order it was clear the man was taking the back roads in the direction of Savannah. Once in Georgia, he could easily access Interstate 95 and head further south or get lost in a more populated city area. Kevin gave Mac an update as the Mercedes approached the bridge over the Savannah River towards the city.

"Did you get the license plate number of the Mercedes?" Mac asked.

"Of course, Mac. I live next door to an ex-cop, don't I?" Kevin replied.

He gave the information to Mac along with the color and model of the car. At that point, Mac told him to discontinue following Porter or whoever was driving. There was no longer any point. They could pick him up later using the information Kevin provided.

Kevin was able to turn around before reaching the bridge, which was fine by him. He was just a bit bridge phobic as it turned out, and this particular bridge looked a bit daunting.

Mac called Percy to let him know that the man they presumed to be Porter appeared to have taken flight.

"If that's the case, it may mean that Bartholomew thing is over, as well," Percy pointed out.

"Could be. No way to be certain at this point. I'd like to be able to give Nathan Chadwick the all clear, but even that is dicey," Mac said.

"Do you plan to have the Georgia police pull the Mercedes over?" Percy asked.

"On what grounds?"

"The threats to Hortense come to mind."

"It's one thing when it's in the same state and particularly the same county, but in another state, it's difficult to get the authorities to pay much attention to a charge like that."

"Mac, I'm getting a headache," Percy said.

"Me, too. Let's talk later."

Chapter 41

Harry Bartholomew was no more. It simply had to be that way. Early on he had served his purpose but he had become a liability to Franklin Porter. Moreover, he had become a target for someone using the name Ruby Wilder, who was yet to name her terms. But she was definitely after some sort of settlement with Harry Bartholomew, not Franklin Porter.

So, Franklin Porter he would be again just briefly, until he could find a place to rest long enough decide on who to become next, where to call home and what project to tackle. Normally, he would have had that planned out long ago, but these were not normal times. Other people had seized control and he didn't even know who they were.

Franklin Porter had stopped in Savannah just long enough to have a meal and then headed out onto the interstate headed north. He had reliable contacts in places like Charlotte, Richmond and D.C. and felt comfortable in those surrounds. He might spend one night on the road and then find a place to settle in for a while in one of those places. Or he might even find himself as far north as Newport. There was something calming about the rugged coast of Newport that soothed his soul. Besides, he loved the opulent life it represented.

He really owed Carl a call. Carl needed to disentangle with Sawgrass and do it quietly, before he got in trouble. If anyone went down for the murder of the girl, it would likely be Carl. Particularly since there was no Harry Bartholomew. Just ask anyone. There was no Harry Bartholomew. He'd seen to that.

"Carl, here."

"Carl, it's me."

"Yes, sir."

"Cut the 'sir' shit. You need to make your exit. Things have gotten out of hand," Porter said.

"In what way?" Carl asked.

"I can't go into details, but everything is over. You need to move on. You won't be hearing from me again."

"Wait a minute, you son of a…"

Porter didn't hear the rest of that phrase and was rather glad he didn't. He had grown somewhat fond of Carl, if not the other people who had worked for him from time to time. He certainly wished him no harm, so he thought he owed him that one call, but certainly nothing else.

It was nearly four hours before he reached the North Carolina state line. He looked disdainfully at the rundown South of the Border amusement area to his right. At one point, he had vowed to make enough money to buy it, simply to tear it down. He thought it a blight on America. Not now. Now he had more important goals to pursue and he had for the first time hit an impediment he couldn't have anticipated.

It was then his cell phone rang. He noted that it wasn't Carl. He had programmed his phone to immediately terminate any call from his former "partner". He didn't recognize the number but was afraid not to answer. He didn't really know why.

"Hello."

"Where you off to, Harry?" the Ruby voice said. "It's not like you to run from trouble, is it? You must think I'm trouble, Harry. Do you, Harry? Anyway, you're going in the right direction. We'll settle up when you get here. See you soon."

Porter was shaken as he pulled the Mercedes over to the side of the busy highway. He knew immediately that was a mistake, as a North Carolina Highway Patrol car pulled up right behind him lights flashing.

"What's the problem, sir?" the officer said, as he approached the window Porter had rolled down.

"Nothing really, officer, I just felt a little lightheaded for a moment," Porter replied, "I seem to be fine now."

As expected, the officer asked for his license and documentation, but Porter was fully prepared. After some discussion, the officer seemed convinced that he was alright and waved him on. Porter was relieved he didn't have to suffer the indignity of a sobriety test.

After driving on for only a few miles, he decided to find the nearest reasonable hotel, turn off his phone and try to get a good night's sleep. He was beginning to believe he was losing his mind. How could the caller possibly know that he was traveling and for that matter in which direction. Impossible, he thought. But if it was impossible …, could it be that the call never happened? Was he imagining everything?

Porter saw a billboard advertising a Marriott only a few exits ahead and decided to head there for the evening. It advertised a restaurant on premise which suited him perfectly as he had no inclination to go searching for food or drink.

After checking in an arranging for an upgrade to a reasonably nice suite, he headed to the lobby to find dinner. Finding the menu at the restaurant to his liking, he ordered a cocktail and finally began to relax just a little. The calm wouldn't last, as his cell phone rang again. He recognized the number as that of the call from earlier. He quickly turned off the phone and ordered another drink.

"Make it a double," he said, out of necessity.

Chapter 42

"Mr. Burns … or Detective Burns … or whoever you are. This is Carl Munson. I think we need to talk again. There's been an unforeseen development. Please give me a call as soon as you can."

Mac was quite surprised by the message on his machine. He assumed talks with Carl Munson had come to an end. The man seemed, as Percy noted, resolute.

"Carl, this is Mac Burns. Where would you like to meet?"

"Your call, sir. I'm at a disadvantage this time, I think," Carl Munson responded.

"Alright then, let's plan on meeting at the law office tomorrow morning at 10AM. Percy has an office there and if Ms. Mendendo is available, she may wish to join us, if needed."

"I'll be there, God willing," Munson replied.

Mac wasn't certain what he meant by 'God willing', but it sounded a bit foreboding. He checked with Percy and found out that both he and Hortense would be in the office and that the meeting could be in Hortense's office.

At 10AM sharp the front desk announced that one Carl Munson had arrived and was waiting to meet with Mac.

"Send him to my office," Hortense responded.

"Carl, we appreciate you coming in," Mac said, offering his hand.

Munson almost reluctantly accepted the handshake.

"You remember, Percy … and this is Ms. Hortense Mendendo, Esquire, a partner of this firm," Mac explained.

Carl simply grunted in acknowledgement. He was dressed as Mac and Percy had last seen him, in blazer and slacks with an open collar. Mac was gratified he didn't look out of place in the law offices. It made whatever he was about to divulge more believable, he figured. At least that's the way it always played out in the interrogation rooms he frequented as a police officer.

"Well, Mr. Munson, can we suppose that it's your time to switch sides?" Mac asked, half sarcastically.

"I'm afraid it's a bit more complicated than that, Mr. Burns. My team has for all intents and purposes disbanded."

Mac, Percy and Hortense all glanced at each other, not fully understanding what they were hearing or the implications.

"I beg your pardon?" Mac said.

"Well, to a large extent, my team was simply me and a man named Harry Bartholomew. Oh, there were two other men at first and we incorporated the help of a guy named Nathan Chadwick for a while, but they have all disappeared or been disappeared."

"Been disappeared?" Percy repeated.

"Hell, I don't even know what that means. All I know is, they aren't around anymore," Carl said, "But knowing Harry, when you aren't needed any more, he makes sure the separation is clean … if you know what I mean."

"Then what about you?" Mac asked.

"I got a call from him yesterday telling me to bail out of Sawgrass to save my ass, but I'm of the opinion that the other shoe hasn't dropped."

"Thus the 'God willing'," Mac said.

"Exactly," Carl said.

"So, that's why you're here?" Hortense asked, "To seek safe haven?"

"Well, that and to help you bring him down, if I can."

"At what cost to the justice system?" Hortense asked, looking at him warily.

"Just a fair shake, when all the truth comes out."

"Truth about extortion?" Percy asked.

"Yes, but we really didn't get very far with that, did we?" Carl pointed out.

"And one or more murders?" Mac got right to the point.

"Well, I suppose I can help you with one of those," Carl admitted.

"Again, for a price, I assume?" Hortense pursued her line of questioning.

"Yes, ma'am … but not too dear."

"Look, Carl, we are most interested in whether the girl—Ruby Wilder—is dead. Did you kill her and if so, at who's instruction?" Mac pressed.

"Here is the God's honest truth. I don't know if she is dead. I assume so, but don't know definitively. When we dumped her body into the Savannah River, she was heavily drugged. I had no stomach for actually killing the girl. But I supposed she didn't have much chance of surviving. It's like the old death by firing squad, some men had live rounds and some not, because some couldn't stand the thought of killing someone. That's me. So, to this day, I hold out hope the cold water woke her up and she swam to safety."

"Was she bound?" Mac asked.

"No, absolutely not," Carl replied, raising his voice slightly.

"So, your hope is the only thing you might be charged with, other than anything related to extortion, is attempted murder, am I guessing right?" Percy asked, dusting off his best attorney attitude.

"I guess, but I know a lot depends on finding a body or not, or whether she turns up. Still, I'm smart enough to know that convicting for murder without a body is a stretch."

"But we have a confession," Mac said.

"Off the record, unfortunately. No recording, unfortunately," Hortense pointed out.

"Okay, then, Carl, give me an example of how you can help us," Mac said.

"Well, one way is keeping you posted of where he is at all times."

"What? How do you do that?" Percy asked.

"I was his technology guy. That assignment included setting up his phones. And when I say phones, I mean phones. He had at least three iPhones at any one time. But I set up all of them and each has a tracing feature, so that I can keep track of him. He's on his way up Interstate 95 right now. I can pinpoint his location precisely, but we'll need to chat a bit more before I do."

"Fascinating!" Percy proclaimed.

"Did Bartholomew know you were doing that?" Mac asked.

"Of course not," Carl responded. "You always have an ace up your sleeve."

"Anybody else have access to this information?" was Mac's next question.

"Again, we'll need to talk a bit more about our working arrangement before I tell you that. I'm sure you understand," Carl said.

"Just one more way you might be able to assist us today, Carl," Mac said, pulling his iPhone from his pocket.

He retrieved the picture he took of Franklin Porter in the restaurant and showed it to Carl Munson.

"Is this a picture of Harry Bartholomew?" Mac asked.

"Of course, it is," Carl said without hesitation. "Yep, that's Harry."

Chapter 43

Things being as they were, Hortense saw no sense in trying to hold Carl in custody, even though he had confessed to dumping a still breathing Ruby Wilder into the river. No, he needed to stay close to them and she was confident he wouldn't run. She instructed him to go home and await further instructions. He left after hesitating only a moment to consider the freedom he was being offered.

"That was mighty magnanimous of you, Hortense," Mac said.

"He's not going anywhere. And I'm not ready to recommend that the DA make him a deal."

"Mac, I guess we should reconnect with Nathan Chadwick now," Percy said. "He needs to know that the man that he knows as Bartholomew is himself on the run. I guess he can come back if he wants."

"I suppose so. No reason to continue spending the firm's money on hotel expenses," Mac agreed.

Mac and Percy excused themselves and went to Percy's office to call the Sawgrass executive. Mac rang the number of Nathan Chadwick's burner phone.

"Hello … is that you Burns?"

"Nathan, I think I have good news for you."

"How's that?" Chadwick said.

"Bartholomew is on the run himself. Something spooked him and he pulled up roots and left town," Mac explained.

"You're kidding! Are you sure? He's pretty smart. Maybe he's just in hiding."

"No, we have a reliable source who is monitoring his every move," Mac responded, even as he nearly choked on the words 'reliable source'.

"Well, I'll be damned."

"So, gather up your wife and head on back home. We'll bring you up to date when you get back," Mac said.

"About my wife … seems like she's left me."

"What? What the hell happened?" Mac said, his voice raising half a tone.

"She somehow knew about Ruby and it wasn't pleasant when she got here."

"I'll bet."

"I convinced her to stay a couple of days and did my best to rationalize, but nothing worked. I think she already has an attorney because she went outside to use her phone a couple of times."

"Well, come back to town anyway. I don't think there's anything to fear from Bartholomew. Maybe your wife, but not Bartholomew."

"How about charges?" Chadwick asked.

"We'll deal with that when you get here, but you won't be arrested immediately, if that's what you mean."

Mac filled in the blanks for Percy before deciding to head home for the day. He was about halfway home when his cell phone rang. It was Carl Munson.

"Burns."

"It's Carl. He's changed course."

"I'm sorry?"

"Bartholomew has changed course. He's now heading west on I-40 and nearing I-85."

"Damn … listen, Carl … this is really important. If he gets onto I-85 I need to know if he goes north or south."

"Got it. I'll call you right away."

Southbound on I-85 would put Atlanta dead ahead for Franklin Porter aka Harry Bartholomew. Mac didn't like the feel of that. He didn't want to think that Nathan Chadwick was back in harm's way, but he remembered what Carl Munson had said about Batholomew's former associates being "disappeared".

All the variables went through his head. How in the world could Porter know Chadwick was in the Atlanta area? Even if he did, how could he find him in that large metropolitan region? What connections had he missed?

He'd wait until he heard back from Munson before calling Chadwick again.

Fifteen minutes later his phone rang again.

"Yes?"

"South … he's headed south."

"Damn. Thanks, Carl."

Mac felt as though he had no alternative but to call Nathan Chadwick right away. It seemed almost impossible that Porter was on Chadwick's trail but it wasn't the time to take chances. It was time to wrack his brain to figure out what he had missed.

"Hello?"

"Nathan, it's Mac. Are you packed and ready to go?"

"Not yet. I didn't think there was any hurry. Figured I'd check out in the morning."

"I suggest you head on out today."

"What's the hurry?" Chadwick asked, his voice beginning to sound a bit shaky.

"Batholomew is heading south on I-85. Probably means nothing, but I don't like it."

"If you don't like it, I don't like it. I'm out of here."

"Good. The sooner the better. Call me from the road," Mac closed off the call.

When Mac got home, he decided to take a multipronged approach to finding out what he had missed along the way. He needed to start by trying to find out if Ruby Wilder was actually dead. He called Carl and got him to agree to take him to the spot where he had dumped her body the following morning. He then called Percy and asked him to run some checks on Ruby in her hometown … last place of residence, her college experience … anything he could find out about her past or present.

If Ruby had survived, he figured, she might have gone back home, hoping to stay alive and out of the clutches of the men who had tried to kill her in the first place. Maybe she would turn up.

The next morning Mac and Carl met at a place not far from the spot on the riverbank where Carl and Nicholas had dragged the girl's body in a half open body bag and pushed it into the water. Carl had made sure that the body bag was half open just in case the girl woke up and could swim away.

Mac walked several hundred feet along the banks in the direction of the water's flow looking for any sign that someone might have crawled out of the water, but saw nothing obvious in the overgrowth, twigs and garbage along the river's edge.

He started to turn back when Carl spoke.

"Wait, Mac," Carl said, cupping his hand above his eyes to curtail glare.

"What?" Mac said looking in that direction.

"Look at the tree. What is that snagged on it? I think it could be the body bag," Carl replied.

"Come on, Carl, that could be anything."

"Maybe, but it sure looks like it."

"I think it might be wishful thinking on your part," Mac challenged him.

"Could be, but I'm almost tempted to swim out there."

"Don't even think about it … look at that current."

"And that's what the Wilder girl would have been dealing with, if she woke up at all," Carl said, head down.

"But she was considerably younger than you. So, there's a chance she got out."

Mac couldn't quite figure out why he was being conciliatory. It wasn't like him, but Carl's obvious pain had an impact.

"Let's get out of here, Carl, I don't think we can draw any conclusions based on what we're seeing or not seeing today."

Mac headed home, and as soon as he walked in the door Percy was on the phone with the first results.

"No one has seen or heard from her in months, but here's something interesting. In college, she was a champion swimmer."

"Well, I'll be damned," Mac said, shaking his head.

Chapter 44

Nathan Chadwick was once again a "rabbit", or at least that's what he thought of himself. Running scared from a beast in an expensive suit. Yet again he reviewed the sequence of events that had led to him to this place. Now he had lost his wife, his mistress, likely his job, maybe his freedom and most of all his self-respect. Maybe his life was next. Should he even go back home, he wondered? Maybe he should just keep driving. But to where? To what end?

For the moment he would just let the road lead him. Yes, that's it. Let the road determine where he would be. And somewhere on I-75 heading south towards Macon, Georgia, the road decided he would be … nowhere. Nathan Chadwick died in a ditch at precisely 4:30 in the afternoon.

"So, we still don't know conclusively if Ruby Wilder is dead," Mac said.

Mac, Percy and Shelby were sitting on Mac's front porch having a late afternoon drink and discussing the matter at hand.

"Nothing at the riverbank made me think someone made it out," Mac continued, "And when Carl and I were there the current was very strong. Even if the girl was a powerful swimmer, if she was the least bit groggy, it would have been pretty tough to get out."

"But not impossible?" Shelby asked, seeming to hold on to a shred of hope.

"No, I suppose nothing is impossible," Mac said.

"Have you heard anything from Chadwick yet?" Percy asked.

"No, I haven't," Mac responded, "I guess I'll give him a call."

Mac got the standard "not available message". He tried again several minutes later and got the same response.

"That's a little odd," Mac said, "But maybe he forgot to charge his phone or something. I guess he'll turn up sooner or later."

Nathan Chadwick did in fact turn up later that night, but he turned up on the eleven o'clock news.

"Local resident and Sawgrass Electrical Cooperative President Nathan Chadwick died today in a one car accident on Interstate 75. Police say Chadwick was traveling alone and apparently lost control of his car and ran off the side of the highway into a deep ravine. Mr. Chadwick's wife, Sharon, said the executive had been in Atlanta on business and was returning home."

The report was accompanied by pictures of the car clearly overturned and police and rescue vehicles on the scene.

The news caught Mac by surprise. He found it unlikely that Franklin Porter had anything to do with Chadwick's death, but the timing was very coincidental. It was also bad news for the Beaufort County district attorney, since he felt certain Chadwick would have made a good witness. Now it became important that they protect Carl Munson.

Shelby had stayed with Mac since her shift the next day was for dinner service. Those were always Mac's favorite nights, since sleep took a backseat to lovemaking.

The next morning Mac called Hortense to make sure she was aware of Chadwick's death. She was and had told Percy.

Mac now felt it was time to focus fully on Franklin Porter. He figured it was a good bet that the blood of Ben Parker, Ruby Wilder, and maybe even Nathan Chadwick, were on his hands and he needed to be brought down. To find him, he needed Carl Munson's help.

"Carl, it's Mac."

"Hello, Mac. What can I do for you?" Carl responded.

"First of all, I guess you heard that your old boss is dead?"

"Bartholomew?"

"No, Nathan Chadwick."

"Hell, no, I hadn't heard. What happened?"

"They say he drove off the side of I-75," Mac told him.

"I'll be damned."

"Listen, can you tell me where Bartholomew is now?" Mac asked.

"Sure … he's stationary in Atlanta."

Carl was able to pinpoint Porter's location with GPS accuracy much to Mac's surprise. Mac recognized the area of midtown. Kevin's earlier surveillance of Porter's house in Palmetto Bluff had yielded information about his car, a late model Mercedes, including license plate.

Mac decided to call his former partner Barney Felton with Atlanta Police Department for a potential assist. Barney was now a detective and still a year away from retirement. They had been beat cops together and had become fast friends. Mac had called on Barney for assistance a couple of times since his retirement and Barney never failed to point out that he was no longer a police officer and should be enjoying sitting under a palm tree somewhere … where he hoped to be shortly.

"Detective Felton."

"Well, don't you sound all official?" Mac kidded.

"Just how did I know it was going to be you, Mac …
just how did I know?" Barney kidded right back.

"How ya been, partner?" Mac asked.

"Hangin' in there, Mac, but I'm afraid to ask what I can
do for you. I'm afraid you'll tell me."

"This favor is something you do best. I want you to
arrest someone."

"Excuse me? Last time I checked you were in South
Carolina and retired and I'm in Georgia trying to enforce
the law."

"There's a man there in midtown who is wanted on suspicion of three murders and attempted extortion here in
Beaufort County. He's a slippery son of bitch and I need
him in someone's custody as soon as possible."

"I see. Well, fax or email me some paperwork from the
DA along with his name and location and we can pick him
up and hold him temporarily, I guess, Barney said.

"Well, Barney, the truth is the paperwork may take a
little time. He hasn't been charged yet, but will be soon,"
Mac explained.

"Then what the hell would I arrest him for—vagrancy?"
Barney said, laughing out loud.

"Look, Barney, just pull him in for questioning about
the death of one Ruby Wilder in Bluffton, South Carolina.
I can email you enough particulars so that you can hold him
for interrogation while I get him charged. It's just important
that we get him off the street before he just disappears."

Barney was silent for a good while.

"This had better be good, Mac. Give me the details and
we'll bring him in. But we can't hold him long."

"Thanks, Barney. This is one bad dude."

Chapter 45

Things were beginning to heat up. Before ending the call, Mac gave Barney the information about Porter's location along with a description of his car and license plate number in case he was on the move again. He then placed a call to Hortense to ask her to get in touch with Beaufort County District Attorney Gil Brandon. That would get the ball rolling in preferring charges against Franklin Porter, aka Harry Bartholomew, in the death of Ruby Wilder and the attempted extortion of Sawgrass Electric Co-op.

Mac remembered Brandon as an ambitious man and one who believed in the rule of law. He also remembered that Hortense seemed to have a reasonable amount of influence over him. At least, he respected her legal opinion, so would likely take her advice on the charges once they had a chance to meet. Up until now, Ruby Wilder had been considered a missing person, but Hortense would need to explain to Brandon that they had reason to believe that she was indeed deceased.

Something Mac heard the night before was sticking in his mind. Sharon Chadwick had told the authorities that her husband had been on a business trip to Atlanta and was returning home. Was that just to protect his reputation? Or was there another reason?

Mac called Carl once more to tell him to stand by and to ask if Porter had changed locations.

"Is he still in that same area of Atlanta?" Mac asked.

"Yep … just hunkered down it looks like," Carl responded. "Nowhere to go, I guess."

"Listen, Carl, I think charges are going to be brought against Bartholomew soon, so be prepared to testify against him. It's your best chance to get a good deal out of this thing."

"I know. I'm not going anywhere."

Hortense called Mac an hour later with some slightly disappointing news. Gil Brandon agreed to meet with her, but not until the next morning. So, any paperwork would be delayed. Barney might have difficulty holding onto Porter more than 24 hours.

As if on cue, Barney called.

"Hello, Barney."

"Hello, Mac. I've got an update for you, but it's not going to be what you expected. The car was pulled over in the general area that you gave us. Like you said, late model Mercedes. The plates matched exactly. But here's the thing. It was a woman driving. Not the guy you described. We had to let her go, of course."

Mac was stunned. His first thought was to call Carl to see if Porter was still stationary. If they hadn't seen the car first and given that he had been in midtown, pinpointing a specific hotel was virtually impossible. The officers would have had to canvas several no doubt. With that on his mind, he thanked Barney and made that call. Carl informed him that the man he knew as Bartholomew was still at the same location.

Mac was now totally confused, but realized he had forgotten one thing. He didn't ask Barney for the woman's name. He called Barney back.

"Yes, Mac."

"I've lost my instincts as a cop, Barney. Who was the woman driving the car?"

"Let me look it up here," Barney replied.

"Says here on the officer's report, it was a woman named Sharon Chadwick, from Bluffton, South Carolina."

That information sent Mac's mind reeling. Sharon Chadwick? How in world did she factor into this? How in the world did she know Porter or Bartholomew? How did she end up with his car?

Mac realized Barney was still talking.

"I guess since the car had South Carolina plates, it all looked perfectly normal."

"What about the registration?" Mac asked. It would have been routine to ask to see it.

"Well, you know, the report doesn't mention them specifically asking for it. That's bad," Barney admitted, "And I guess it never occurred to this idiot cop that she may have stolen the damned car."

"Yes, sir, that is bad. She must be attractive then," Mac said with resignation.

"I guess. Damnit. He'll get a rip for this," Barney said, clearly disgusted by the officer's mistake.

"Barney, there is a meeting with the Beaufort County District Attorney in the morning to try to get paperwork done and an arrest warrant sworn out. As far as we know, this guy is still holed up in midtown. We have a way of tracking him. So, once I have the warrant, I may need some more help. You game?"

"Once you have the warrant."

"Fair enough."

"But, Mac, the next time you call, I hope it's strictly for social reasons," Barney said, realizing that was a tall order.

"I'll try to keep that in mind," Mac replied and signed off until the next day.

Sharon Chadwick had Mac completely stumped. She hadn't been a player in any part of this. Connecting the dots was growing increasingly difficult. He knew he had to talk with her one way or another. It might involve having the Beaufort County police help by pulling her over, if and when she returns to the area. After all, technically she was driving a stolen car.

Burt Justin was now Chief of Police in Beaufort County. He'd come up through the ranks and was well liked by the men and women under his command. Mac had met him through Hortense and they had lunch on occasion to share cop stories and escapades of days playing college football.

Mac gave Burt a call and explained the situation with Franklin Porter's car and the fact that Sharon Chadwick now seemed to be in possession.

"It's a bit of a ticklish situation, Mac. Sure, we can pull her over and ask some questions, but the woman just lost her husband and up 'til now, has been a respected member of the community. At least as far as I know. Maybe we can just take this a little slowly," Burt suggested.

"Afraid of the optics, Burt?" Mac asked.

"Frankly, yes. Those types of things make the entire area a bit squeamish. Maybe we pull her over and ask her to come in on her own. If she doesn't show up, then we have more reason to actually arrest her."

"Makes sense to me," Mac admitted.

"Okay, we'll be on the lookout for her and cruise by her residence a few times a day as well," Burt said.

"Thanks, my friend. Next lunch is my treat," Mac said.

"I'll hold you to that."

Chapter 46

Downstream from the city of Savannah, Georgia, the Savannah River broadens into an estuary before flowing into the Atlantic Ocean. The area where the river's estuary meets the ocean is known as Tybee Roads. There in the brackish waters, a fisherman found the body of Ruby Wilder. Of course, he didn't know who she was and it took local authorities several days to make the determination and link her back to the missing person in Beaufort County in next door South Carolina.

Mac heard the news from Percy just about the time Gil Brandon had agreed to issue the warrant for Franklin Porter. Ruby's confirmed death did create a new problem, however. Brandon was now insisting on bringing in and charging Carl Munson for her murder. Hortense was trying her best to slow down that process according to Percy, but Gil seemed determined.

It served no particular purpose to warn Carl, Mac figured. He'd probably run. It would make convicting Porter more difficult if Carl didn't cooperate.

Hortense managed to get a copy of the warrant for Franklin Porter, scanned and emailed it to Mac, who in turn emailed it to Barney. He called his old partner shortly thereafter.

"Hello, Mac," Barney answered.

"Is that sufficient for you to pick up Porter?" Mac asked.

"That works, Mac, but it may take time. There are six hotels within four blocks of the position you specified and fourteen just a few blocks further out. I can't afford to put ten officers on it. Maybe two, at most, so it may take time."

"Just do the best you can, Barney, that's all I can ask."

"I'll call you, if and when we have him."

"Thanks, Barney," Mac said, ending the call.

That evening Shelby and Percy both joined Mac on his front porch for drinks. Mac brought them up to date on the odd turn of events with Sharon Chadwick, and clearly noticed Shelbys sadness about Ruby Wilder's confirmed death.

"She didn't deserve that, Mac," Shelby said, "You need to nail that bastard."

"It's all in process, Shelby. The district attorney is working on it and Barney is looking for him in Atlanta right now. It's only a matter of time 'til we have him," Mac promised.

At about 6PM, Burt Justin called with an update.

"Mac, Sharon Chadwick finally showed up and we pulled her over near her home. Things got a little sticky for a few minutes. The cops that pulled her over noticed some duffle bags in her back seat and just asked her what was in them. She asked out of blue, if they had a warrant."

"That seems a little bit strange. They hadn't asked to search the bags, had they?" Mac asked.

"No. But her question seemed to raise their suspicions. They asked her to step out of the car. At that point, they said they had probable cause for drugs and opened the first bag."

"And?"

"It wasn't drugs—it was money—lots of money," Burt said.

"Where is she now?"

"We're kind of stuck now. She's in the lockup for the moment, while we try to find the right judge to make a determination if we let her out on bail, if we even have an appropriate charge, and so on and so forth. What a mess," Burt admitted.

"I assume you'll confiscate the money until you find out the source?" Mac asked.

"We have no choice."

"Okay, I hate to ask," Mac said, "but please keep me posted, no matter what time it is. We're on the verge of arresting Franklin Porter in Atlanta. At least, I think we are."

"It's irregular—but will do."

"Holy shit!" Mac said to Percy and Shelby

He further explained what he had just learned, and wondered out loud if the money, like the car, had come from Franklin Porter. The three discussed it for a few more minutes, decided to order Chinese for dinner, and mixed another drink. It seemed like the logical course of action.

At that point, Mac's cell phone rang again.

"Mac," Mac said, assuming it was Burt again.

"Mac, did you send the cops?" Carl said.

"Carl? What are you saying?"

"They're outside and they act like they plan to arrest me," Carl said, sounding amazingly calm.

"No, Carl, I didn't send them, but you'd best just go along," Mac advised.

"Not a chance in hell, pal. I have another way out of here and I plan to use it. See you on the flip side, Mr. Detective."

Bad sign, Mac thought.

After enjoying their Chinese dinner, Mac and Shelby decided to retire for the evening and binge watch some old Law and Order reruns. Shelby loved to tease Mac about that habit given his background, but she had come to enjoy

watching with him and saw why Sam Waterston had become his favorite actor.

Burt never called back that evening, so Mac assumed
that Sharon Chadwick was the guest of the Beaufort County lockup for the night. Serves her right for mouthing off,
he supposed. But it turned out he was in for another surprise. His cell phone rang at 10:30. It was Barney.

"Do you have him, Barney?"

"Not exactly, Mac. But we do have his phone."

"What?" Mac said, not believing his ears.

"We found the room he'd been staying in. He had never
checked out but there were no clothes or other personal
effects left in the room, only his cell phone."

"That probably means he knew he was being tracked or
didn't want to be. He's in the wind now. Damn it."

"We did our best, Mac. Sorry," Barney said.

"Not your fault—a day late and … you know."

"At least we can bag the phone and send it to your PD
in Beaufort."

"Thanks, Barney."

"Good night, Mac."

"Good night, Barney."

Chapter 47

As Mac lay awake in his bed that night, Shelby sleeping peacefully beside him, he took stock of where they were. Franklin Porter, aka Harry Bartholomew, was on the run, Carl Munson was on the run, Ruby Wilder was confirmed dead, Nathan Chadwick was dead and the only person in jail was perhaps the one least likely to end up there—the widow of Chadwick.

Sharon Chadwick hadn't been on anyone's radar at all, least of all his. Then out of the blue, she turns up with Franklin Porter's car and a bunch of money in duffle bags, spouting attitude at the local police. Just doesn't add up, he thought. Had she somehow confronted Porter? If so, why? How was she even aware of him? How would she even find him? Puzzling to be sure. There must be a common link.

Think, Mac, think. You're missing something. You have been for a while.

Mac bounded out of bed the next morning and was happy to find Shelby making breakfast. He kissed her on the cheek and promised to be in to sit down and enjoy it right after making a quick call.

"Beaufort Police Department. How can I help you?"

"Can I speak with Chief Justin, please?"

"Who can I say is calling, sir?" the officer asked.

"It's Mac Burns, retired detective from Atlanta. He knows me."

"Yes, sir."

It was only a minute or two before Burt came to the phone.

"Hello, Mac."

"Morning, Burt. Do you still have the Chadwick woman?"

"So far, but we have to find a judge quickly. We're running out of time to hold her on suspicion."

"I know this will strike you as a strange question, but is there some way that I can be permitted to ask her some questions—maybe acting as a consultant to the force or something."

"Come on, Mac, you know better. What do you want to know from her?"

"By now, I'm sure you know the car is registered to Franklin Porter, right?"

"Yep. We checked."

"Then the questions are pretty simple, I guess. How does she know Franklin Porter and how did she find him in Atlanta?"

"Look Mac, we can ask her those questions. But it won't be long before we have to release her."

"Okay. It's important to try to get those answers, if possible."

Mac and Shelby hadn't even finished breakfast when Burt called Mac back.

"Mac, Mrs. Chadwick claims she never heard of any Franklin Porter, and by the way she answered, I'm inclined to believe her. And with that answer, the second one seemed kind of irrelevant, don't you think?"

"I guess so. Thanks, Burt."

Mac thought for a minute and then explained what had just happened to Shelby.

"Supposing the chief is right, Mac, and she's never heard of Porter. What's the significance of that?" Shelby asked.

"I had to think about it, but it probably means she went to midtown Atlanta to confront Harry Bartholomew!"

"But why?"

"She would have good reason. From her perspective, Bartholomew was tearing their family apart by turning her husband into something he'd never been … a criminal."

"But how would she even know ab   out him?" Shelby asked.

"I have a hunch Nathan Chadwick told her himself. His world was crumbling around him and he was trying to hold onto his family at least. So maybe he was casting blame away from himself, in hopes she would forgive him for various transgressions."

"But I gather she didn't go there to kill him, at least, as far as we know," Shelby pointed out.

"As far as we know. It could be that she decided to hit him where you can always hurt men like that, in the pocketbook. She took him for his money and even his car. Must have thought it was sweet revenge," Mac said.

"And then, she dumps dumbass Nathan after all," Shelby chuckled.

"Sweet revenge yet again," Mac said. "But she didn't figure on the fact that we would have the Atlanta PD be on the lookout for that car. Just luck on our part."

"Not so, Mac. You had it under surveillance even back here at Porter's home."

"Shelby, I have to call Burt back and have him ask her one more question," Mac said.

"How she knows Harry Bartholomew?"

"Right."

Mac quickly found out it was too late to have Burt ask the logical next question. The chief felt that they had no reason to hold Mrs. Chadwick, since no one had reported a stolen car or any stolen cash, at least in his jurisdiction. So, they let her go. Money and all.

Mac was more than a little surprised. He decided to try to find the widow and ask her some questions of his own. Of course, she would be under no obligation to answer them, but perhaps if he used the status of the law firm, it might make an impression. He called Percy and began formulating a plan.

Percy agreed to help.

Chapter 48

Carl had no particular plan for his next stop or what he might do when he got there. When he worked for Bartholomew, he had each day fairly mapped out for him, but now he was on his own. Maybe he'd learned enough from the guy he often called "the invisible man" to run his own scams. Or maybe he'd trade on his own knowledge of information systems and get a straight job. Naw. Bad plan. Limited income potential.

What he did know is that he couldn't completely leave the area until he connected with his lady friend. He liked the sound of that—lady friend. He was much too old to have a "girlfriend". And the woman he was sleeping with was definitely a lady.

Carl Munson drove a late model Chevy Camaro. He also had Ruby's car in a garage in Savannah, but didn't dare drive it yet, for obvious reasons. The Camaro was equipped with a police scanner. As he was driving on Route 46 near the Georgia line, he heard a police conversation about the arrest and then release of one Sharon Chadwick.

Oh, come on, he thought, *not possible. She's too smart for that.*

But it was true. His "lady friend" slipped up in some way and found herself spending the night in the Beaufort jail on some trumped-up charge. Carl immediately tried to call her.

Carl Munson had been seeing Sharon Chadwick nearly every day for months. They had met a day or so after he joined Sawgrass in the senior information systems position replacing Ben Parker. It had happened purely by accident as Sharon had visited Nathan at his office while out shopping one day. Nathan hated having her drop in for whatever reason. Carl ended up walking Sharon to the elevator and out to the parking lot. They stood by her car and talked for most of an hour. Carl wondered why he wasn't missed, but realized his real boss was Bartholomew, so tossed off any worries. Carl and Sharon had much in common they felt and agreed to have lunch the following day at a quiet restaurant in Bluffton. It was small enough and far enough from the co-op offices that Carl figured no one would notice.

The affair blossomed to the point where Carl told Sharon a bit more than he should about the pressure being put on Nathan. Sharon wasn't at all happy to hear that, but seemed unwilling to break off the relationship with Carl. She found it stimulating, if edgy. It was exactly the type of thing she needed at that moment.

Sharon answered Carl's call.

"What, Carl … what do you want?"

Sharon didn't sound like herself. Not herself at all.

"What's the matter with you?" Carl asked.

"What's the matter? What's the matter? I just spent the night in jail, that's what's the matter. A woman of my stature in jail. What the hell is going on in this world, Carl, I ask you?" Sharon replied.

"Where are the kids, Sharon?" Carl asked, genuinely worried.

"With Nathan's parents in Charleston, if you must know," Sharon responded in a huff.

"What did you do to get yourself put into jail?"

"They pulled me over with Bartholomew's car," she answered truthfully.

"Oh shit, please don't tell me you killed the bastard," Carl said, clearly worried.

"No Carl, I didn't kill him. I just persuaded him to part with certain assets."

"Just by talking to him?" Carl said incredulously.

"And with the gun you gave me in my hand."

"That always seems to help."

"Carl, we need to meet and plan what we do next. Get over here," Sharon seemed to order him.

"I can't. They have an arrest warrant out for me for murdering the Wilder chick."

"Oh, just ducky. Then where do we meet?" Sharon asked.

"Okay, meet me in front of the Krispy Kreme at the Tanger in Pooler," Carl suggested.

"Why there?" Sharon asked.

"… 'cause I want a donut, Sharon, why does it matter? By the way, drive your own damned car this time."

The Tanger outlets were right on I95, south of the state line, and meeting there was like hiding in plain sight, Carl figured. Anyway, he was hungry.

When Sharon pulled up, Carl noticed she was driving her normal Volvo. He was relieved that Bartholomew's Mercedes was nowhere to be seen.

"Did you bring the money?" Carl asked.

"I brought half the money," Sharon admitted.

"And how much is that?"

"Nearly a million," Sharon responded.

"And that's an even split?" Carl said sounding suspicious.

"Yes Carl, why would I cheat you?"

"It wouldn't be healthy to do so," Carl pointed out."

"I know you're not violent, Carl."

"I killed a girl."

"I know you didn't mean to," Sharon countered.

Carl was silent.

Chapter 49

Mac was in Hortense's office with Percy. He'd had a bit of a rough night and told Percy he needed to meet with them as early in the morning as possible.

"I think I know what I've been missing," Mac said.

"Do tell," Hortense said.

"I believe Carl Munson has been working with Sharon Chadwick. That's how she knew how to find Franklin Porter and shake him down. That said, I think she only knew him as Harry Bartholomew—the man who was ruining her family."

"So, she shakes down the man who's ruining her family, working in conjunction with the man she's sleeping with, who might also have a hand in ruining her family?" Percy said.

"I didn't say they were necessarily sleeping together. It might just be a partnership of convenience. After all, Carl had a score to settle with Bartholomew, as well," Mac pointed out.

"Point taken," Percy admitted.

"Does your mind always go there, Percy?" Hortense asked.

"Not always … must, most of the time," Percy shrugged.

"Carl was able to keep tabs on the man we know as Porter and feed the information to Mrs. Chadwick, so that she could plan how to exact her revenge," Mac surmised.

"So now we have warrants for Carl and Porter, but not the woman. How do we proceed on that?" Percy asked, "And what charges?"

"I'd say grand larceny is a lock now that we have a pretty good idea of how it all fits together," Mac sad.

"I'll call Gil. I think he'll be okay charging her," Hortense said.

"Have him talk to Burt over at Beaufort PD. They had her for a while and may have more info. I know they checked the registration on the car," Mac said.

Meanwhile, Sharon and Carl were trying to determine whether to stick together or carry on separately, at least for a while. Carl knew he couldn't stay around in the area. Sharon was concerned about being separated from her children for any length of time. She wasn't aware that a warrant might be pending and thought that having been released from custody, she was fairly safe. Neither of them was thinking clearly. Everything had happened too fast. At least now they had money. Money doesn't fix everything, they figured, but it fixes many things.

They agreed that Carl would continue south, and they would reconnect via phone in one week, once Sharon was able to read the situation in Beaufort County. They kissed and Carl headed on.

By the time Sharon arrived home, the Beaufort Police were waiting for her and immediately took her into custody charging her with grand larceny. They, of course, confiscated the money yet again, and it didn't take long to discover that half of it had disappeared. That led to a long session of questioning, but Sharon refused to give Carl up, at least for the moment.

Then came the question.

"How do you know Harry Bartholomew?"

"That worthless son of a bitch tried to drive my husband and family into the ground. Whatever happened to him he deserved," Sharon Chadwick responded.

"What happened to him, ma'am?" the interrogator asked.

"I'm sure I don't know."

"But you have his car."

"He gave it to me."

"And did he give you the money, too?"

"As a matter of fact, he did," Sharon responded.

"Why would he do that?" the officer asked.

"Because I asked him to."

"Did you kill him, Mrs. Chadwick?"

"He was fine when I left him," she responded.

The officer told Sharon Chadwick that they were intrigued by how she might have convinced Bartholomew to meet with her to begin with. She offered no explanation to that at first, other than to say she had called him on more than one occasion. They asked her if she knew that his real name was Franklin Porter, and she again claimed absolutely no knowledge of that fact.

All in all, this former Southern member of country club society showed a newly acquired hard edge brought on presumably by a direct collision with a criminal element, the likes of which she or family and friends had never encountered. She had apparently adapted well. The only softening the officer had noticed was when she asked about her children and their well-being. The officer assured her they were still with her in-laws for the moment and would stay there until things were "sorted out".

It would take more than one sitting to draw the information needed from Sharon Chadwick to locate and bring Carl Munson and Franklin Porter to justice. But they had time and leverage.

Carl had only driven about a hundred miles when his cell phone rang.

"Hello"

"Carl, it's Harry. How are you, my friend?"

"Oh shit, Harry, friend? You must be kidding."

"That aside, Carl, where are you? We should meet and settle up."

"Settle up? What does that mean?"

"I'll explain when we meet. Where are you?" Porter said.

"You must think I'm a fool if you think I'm going to tell you where I am, Harry. I never want to see you again. I'm on my way to somewhere you'll never find me, never think of looking for me."

"There's really no such place, Carl. No such place at all," the voice on the phone said.

"Look, this conversation is going nowhere, Harry, where are you calling from?" Carl tried turning the tables.

"Might be from the car right behind you, Carl. You just never know."

Carl couldn't help but look in his rearview mirror and it caused him to swerve, but he regained control just in time to avoid an accident.

"Clever move, Harry. You trying kill me?" Carl said.

"Not just yet, Carl. Not just yet," Porter said, "What say we just meet further on down the highway. I'll be waiting."

The call ended.

Carl was completely surprised by hearing his old boss's voice again. He assumed Harry Bartholomew had moved on and was out of his life forever. In fact, Harry had told him he was. Could Harry have figured out that he was involved with Sharon Chadwick? Not beyond the realm of possibility, he supposed.

It chilled his soul to think so.

Chapter 50

Franklin Porter supposed he was relieved to find out that the series of calls hadn't come from Ruby Wilder, whether alive or dead. He's never actually met Nathan Chadwick's wife face to face and had no idea why she was so angry with him. Or perhaps he had some inkling. But he was unnerved when she showed up at his hotel room with a gun, demanding revenge by way of money and even his car. He supposed the money was no surprise. After all, everything was about money—but his car?

In reality the thing that pissed him off about the whole affair the most was when she told him that Carl had told her exactly where to find him. In fact, Carl had been tracking his movements for months via his phone. That's how the Chadwick woman was able to intimidate him as he drove up Interstate 95. He had to admit it was a clever plan. Clever, indeed. Carl had even provided her the handgun she now held on him.

Franklin Porter had never been a man of violence. Not personally anyway. Oh, he had had violence delivered upon other people *by* other people, but he himself never raised his hand against anyone, much less a woman. In fact, he supposed he was a coward. So, he had no thought of grabbing for the gun.

He had intended to leave Carl Munson alone, at least for the moment. He'd been a faithful lieutenant after all. But this changed everything. Perhaps he'd give Mr. Munson a dose of his own medicine.

Porter was wise enough not to give the Chadwick woman all his money. Oh, he gave her the contents of the duffle bags he had with him, but within a few paces of the hotel was a Wells Fargo where he could make a withdrawal sufficient to get him on the move again. He decided to rent a car using his new name and head for Memphis where he would check into the Peabody as Marvin Storyman. He'd had the Storyman credentials for a good while. Storyman was a wealthy oil executive from Houston with money to invest. It suited him well.

Yes, he'd settle into the Peabody for a while before finding a new project. But not before haunting Carl to the point of distraction. He himself had felt like he was losing his mind while enduring the Ruby prank. Time to inflict the same sort of fate on his old friend.

Perhaps he'd even give him a call now.

"Hello Carl, where are you now?"

"Fuck off, Harry!"

"Still being coy? I just wanted to tell you how pleasant it was meeting Mrs. Chadwick, notwithstanding losing some spending money. She certainly told me some interesting things about you."

"I don't have any idea what you're talking about."

"You were a bad boy, tracking me all that time … bad boy, indeed. Set me up, in fact."

"Don't call me again, Harry, I mean it!"

"Maybe we'll settle up at the next stop," Porter said laughing.

Carl Munson terminated the call. He pulled the car over at the next rest stop and made another call.

"Mac."

"Mr. Detective. I'm coming in."

Mac couldn't believe his ears. He immediately called Burt Justin at Beaufort PD.

"Burt, surprising as it may seem, Carl Munson is coming in. I think he's likely to turn himself in to me, but I'll bring him in," Mac informed the chief.

"Damn, I didn't see that coming," Burt replied.

"Just a hunch, but I think the thing to do is get him and Sharon Chadwick in the same room, let them see that time has run out, and that they need to help us get Franklin Porter."

"We can do that, if need be," Burt agreed, "just let me know when you have him."

Three hours later, Carl showed up at the law office as Mac instructed him to do. Mac once again showed him into Hortense's office and they were joined by Percy.

"What made you change your mind? And come in, Carl," Mac asked.

"Things are just mounting up and I can't keep running forever. Anyway, Bartholomew was chasing me," Carl responded.

"So, you wanted to come to a place of relative safety?" Percy asked.

"No, I think that problem has been neutralized. At least I think so," Carl said in his normal evasive manner.

"Wait a minute. Did he catch up with you and you managed to kill him?" Mac asked.

"No. I never saw him again, thank goodness. But, if you still want him, I can tell you where he was last time I checked my phone," Carl said, handing Mac a scrap of note paper.

Noting the location, Mac immediately called Burt Justin and began the process of having the police in Tennessee put out a bulletin on Franklin Porter.

"I'm surprised at you, Carl, you just gave up a great deal of your leverage," Mac noted.

"No matter, I know I'm in for a stretch. But I hope you all will remember I co-operated to some degree."

"We'll keep it in mind," Hortense said with a modicum of sincerity.

"I was thinking you could let me plead to a lesser charge on the Wilder thing, maybe manslaughter and let Sharon skate."

"We can't make those decisions, Mr. Munson, but we'll talk to the DA," Hortense assured him.

"Come on Carl, we need to go for a ride," Mac said.

Carl stood up.

"Do I need to ask you if you have a gun?"

"I don't have a gun. I'm a businessman … remember?"

Mac took Carl Munson to the Beaufort Police Department, where he was booked at least initially for manslaughter for the death of Ruby Wilder. At that point not charges were brought for attempted extortion.

Sharon Chadwick was released on bail later that day, and Mac got the impression the district attorney might see fit to recommend probation.

Mac was eating lunch the following day when Burt called him.

"Mac, you won't believe this. The Memphis police found the remains of who they believe to be your Franklin Porter in a fancy suite at the Peabody Hotel in Memphis. He had been burned to death. The coroner has thus far chalked it up to spontaneous human combustion, but the cops don't buy it."

"Why is that?"

"Well one reason is that in all of history there are no fully proven cases of spontaneous human combustion. That makes you wonder. Add to that that his right hand was burned clean off and he had a death grip on his cell phone. Just odd if you ask me," Burt responded.

Mac had his own ideas about the cause of death.

"Damn! Okay, thanks, Burt. Is Munson still in your lockup?"

"So far. He'll likely be moved tomorrow though."

"Alright, I may swing by just for a minute," Mac said.

"See you then."

Mac drove to Beaufort and entered the police station. He easily found his way to the holding cells and saw that Carl Munson was in one of them reading.

"Hello, Carl."

"Ah, hello, Mr. Detective," Carl said mockingly.

"I have news. Your Mr. Bartholomew is dead."

"Do tell," Carl said smiling.

"But then, you knew that didn't you?"

"I'm sure I don't know what you mean."

"You said you thought your problem with Bartholomew had been … what did you say … neutralized?" Mac said.

"I guess, I did."

"Just between us, how did you pull it off?"

"No offense, Mr. Detective, but you don't listen too well, do you? Remember in the law office when I told you he always has at least three phones and I fixed all of them? I just didn't tell you all that I did to them. Sort of slipped my mind. Like I said at the time, ace up my sleeve."

"So, you …?" Mac began to say, then decided to ask no more questions.

Carl Munson would do a great deal of time and Franklin Porter, Hortense's tormentor, was gone. Harry Bartholomew, would-be master criminal, was gone.

Later in Hortense's office, he and Percy were reviewing the case and wrapping up details. Mac had informed Hortense that Porter was deceased, or at least as far as they were able to determine from the burned corpse in the hotel he was. DNA tests were still pending, but it was a good bet, he was gone for good.

"You know one thing about all of this that puzzles me?" Hortense said.

"What's that, Hortense?" Mac asked.

"Why didn't Carl Munson just call you and tell you where Porter was and keep on running? He didn't have to turn himself in."

"That's a keen observation and I would expect nothing less from you. But the answer is, I think, fairly simple. I've spent a fair amount of time with the man and he carries a lot of guilt. He was sincerely hoping Ruby Wilder had made it out of the river alive. But when she didn't, his guilt began to devastate him," Mac said.

"Is that it?" Hortense asked.

"That's not all of it," Mac said, "there's also the Sharon Chadwick angle. I believe he came back, in part, to try to use whatever leverage he had to see to it she got to move on with her life. He felt responsible for her problems, as well."

"That's a lot of guilt to carry," Hortense admitted.

"Anyway, life forever on the run is no way to live," Percy pointed out.

"Based on what I've been told, I think one Franklin Porter could have made it work," Hortense said.

"Maybe so, Ms. Mendendo, just maybe so," Mac nodded his head.

Chapter 51

Mac and Shelby were enjoying a late afternoon drink on Mac's front porch. Joining them this time were Kevin, and of course Hero.

They had an early Jimmy Buffet disc on in the background. Since Jimmy's passing, Shelby had encouraged Mac to get into the troubadour's music as a means of relaxation, tropical style. Mac had to admit it was working to a large degree. But don't dare call him a Parrothead! That would at least earn you a dirty look.

"It's been a few weeks now since that work you did with the law firm, Mac, are you getting bored?" Kevin asked.

"Hell no, I'm not getting bored. Finally, I can become a gentleman of leisure, just as I wanted," Mac said having a sip of his Bombay Sapphire and Tonic.

"Somehow, I just can't see it lasting," Shelby piped in, "it never seems to."

Mac rolled his eyes at the thought. About that time, Percy was pulling up returning from work.

"With your luck, Mac, Percy has some obscure case he needs your help with," Shelby teased.

"Don't even kid about it," Mac said grimacing.

"Hello, fellow travelers!" Percy said, climbing the stairs and reaching down to tousle Hero's ears.

"How was your day?" Mac asked.

"Quite interesting, actually," Percy responded, then looking at Kevin, asked, "Be a good lad and fetch an old man a drink, will you?"

Kevin laughed and replied, "Yes, sire!"

Percy sat down in a porch rocker and considered the mild early evening breeze. He thought he could smell someone cooking out and began considering options for dinner, but grew eager to share his announcement.

"I have what I think is good news. Hortense and I have been talking for several days about my role at the firm. She thinks I bring a good deal of experience and insight, and quite frankly, I've really enjoyed the work," Percy said, accepting a gin and Tonic from Kevin with thanks.

"That's terrific, Percy!" Mac said, almost in tandem with Shelby.

"And here's the thing. She wants me to apply to the South Carolina Bar sooner, rather than later, so that I can join the firm as a full attorney."

"Whoa … that's awesome," Mac said, "What will that take?"

"She thinks because of my … let's say … problem, the firm will have to sponsor me. Then there's actually studying for the test and so forth. But frankly, both she and I think we can pull it off."

"And it's what you want—you're sure?" Mac felt he had to ask.

"Up until recently I wasn't, but I am now. I'm ready to get back to it. I really am," Percy responded, smiling broadly.

"Then I propose a toast to the future Richard Percival, Esquire, Attorney at Law!"

Milton Keynes UK
Ingram Content Group UK Ltd.
UKHW021105200524
442968UK00015B/980

9 798822 942561